HAYLEY REESE CHOW

A CHURN IN THE (VIRTUAL) SOCIETY

Whimsical
Publishing & Illustration

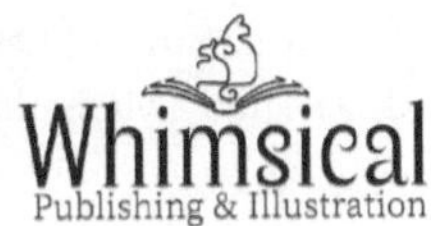

Whimsical Publishing

For information address Whimsical Publishing, whimsicalpublishing.ca

ISBN: 978-1-998195-38-1

Edited by Micheline Ryckman and Deborah O'Carroll
Cover art and Design by Micheline Ryckman

For my VSoc Street Team,
and for all the Belroy boys & babes who shouted into the void,
this one's for you.

MICAH'S INTO THE CHURN SERIES

TIMELINE

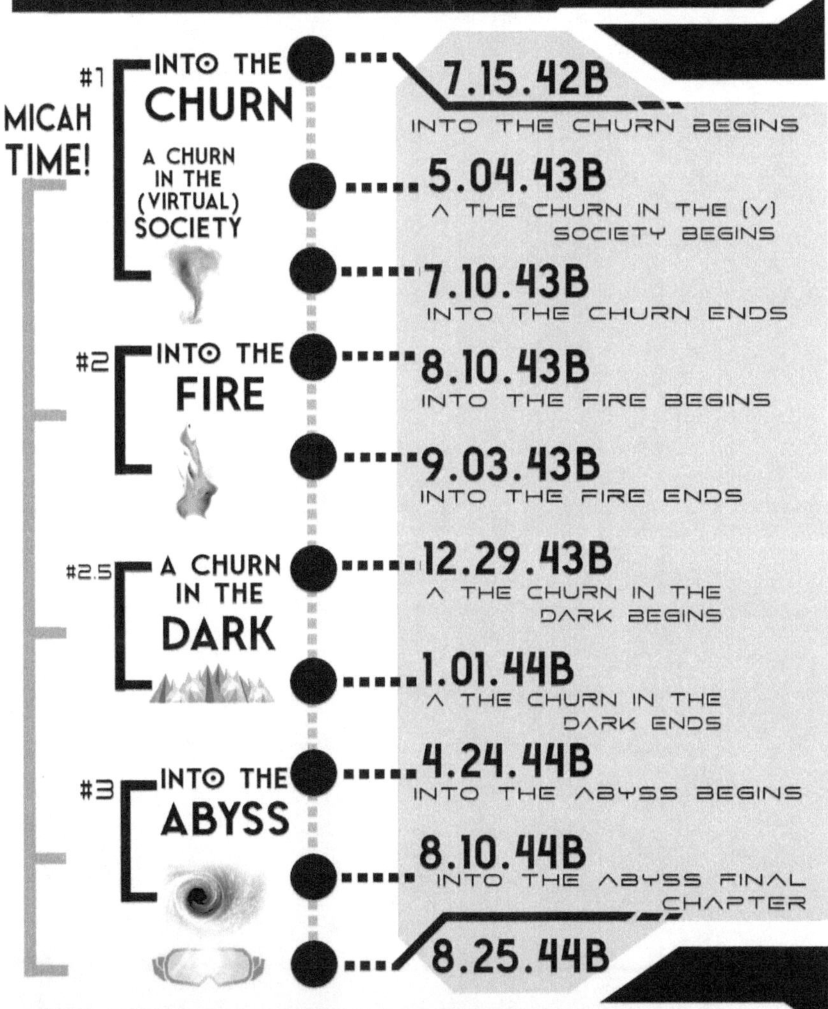

A CHURN IN THE (V) SOCIETY ENDS

Micah's Top-Secret Recap: Beware of Spoilers!

Into the Churn:

After discovering that Calderon was behind the murder of their teammate, Genevieve Navarro, Sterling/Hart won the BRR and used the spotlight to expose Calderon's crimes.

Into the Fire:

After Calderon was wrongfully exonerated, Sterling/Hart traveled to Otho to save Ezren's dad from Baxter Research. There, they found that Baxter had been trafficking the Casolla system's first complex life forms—the luxies—through the system's dark syndicates, and Calderon Industries had been attempting to protect them. Ezren's dad sacrificed himself so Sterling/Hart could save the luxies with help from Calderon's team, though Ambassador York, the syndicate's political front-man, escaped.

A Churn in the Dark:

During Crion's Inaugural Race Royale, a syndicate kingpin known as the Crow left Ambassador York's body on the race royale course and abducted two Belethean royalers in an attempt to manipulate Sterling/Hart into a syndicate partnership. While the Belethean team escaped, they were deeply shaken.

Into the Abyss:

When the syndicate kingpin known as the Crow murdered Calderon, Foster Sterling inherited Calderon Industries and the Crow's unfortunate attention. Foster and Ezren got married and just as Foster was about to assume his CEO responsibilities, he was kidnapped by the Crow. Ezren managed to rescue

Foster, and the Crow tried to blow up the BRR finish line in retaliation. In an epic showdown, Sterling/Hart were able to just barely thwart the terrorist attack and defeat the Crow. With Sterling/Hart taking on new leadership roles, the Casolla system finally seemed to find peace.

.

.

.

.

.

.

But this is the story of what happened between the lines.

MICAH'S INTO THE CHURN SERIES TIMELINE

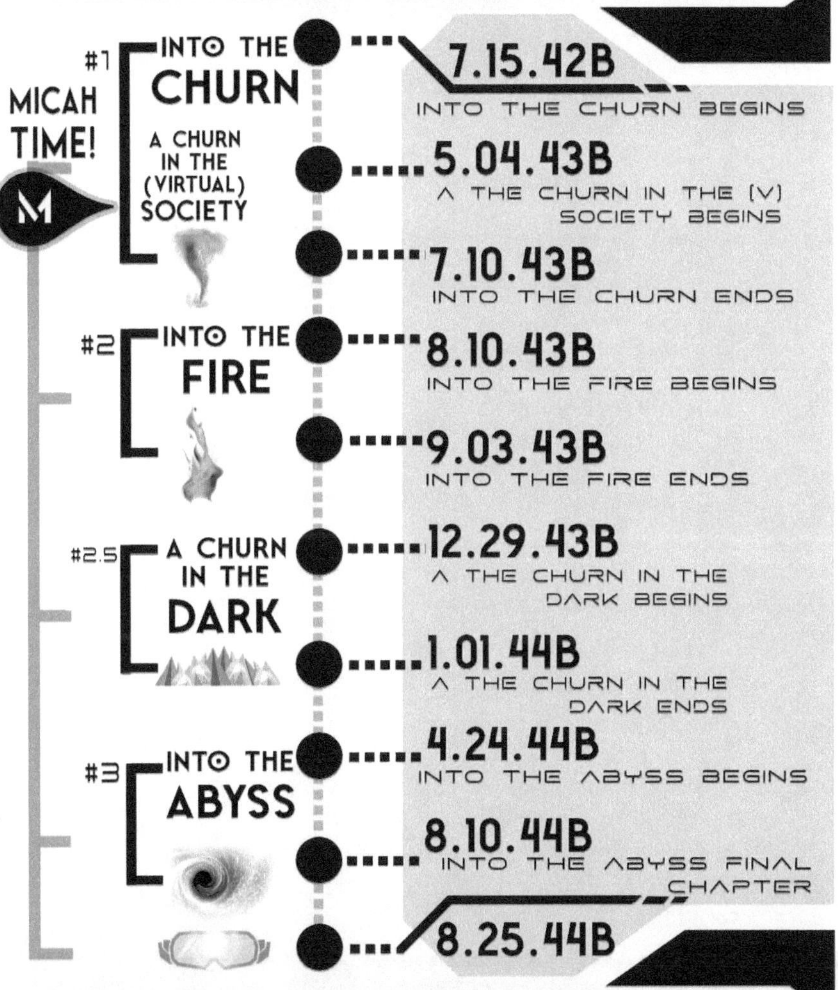

5.04.43B: T-minus 0 days until the BRR

Micah

IT WAS GOING to be the best week of Micah's life—the certainty vibrated in her bones. Alone in her tiny dorm room, Micah squealed for what had to be the hundredth time in the last twenty-four hours, her heart racing as if *she* were about to start the BRR instead of Ezren. A holo of the starting line spilled across her walls, the mauve expanse and jagged, stormy horizon lighting up the otherwise spartan room. Putting the final touches on her VSoc holo, she sent it into the 'verse, blowing it a kiss on its virtual journey. She let the meticulously edited holo play in the dim room, her irises and pigtail buns perfectly matching Team Belethea's teal while the live feed of the starting line provided her background.

Good morning, Belroy boys and babes! This is the day we've been waiting for. Belethea is sending a doubles team to the BRR for the first time in thirty years, and it's our OTP, Sterling/Hart. Not only did

THEY HAVE THE BEST QUALIFIER FINISH IN BELETHEAN HISTORY...

THE HOLO CUT TO THE HIGHLIGHTS OF THEIR DRAMATIC QUALIFIER FINISH, TORNADOES ENCIRCLING THEM AS THEY SPRINTED FOR SAFETY.

BUT AFTER ALL OF YOUR HARD WORK, STERLING/HART FINALLY HAVE THE TOPSUITS THEY DESERVE.

Ezren's and Foster's shocked faces from when Sylvia had surprised them with the suits that morning filled the holo. Ezren's giddy excitement was too cute for words and even Foster had cracked a rare smile.

THANKS TO YOUR RECORD-BREAKING CROWDFUNDING SPRINT, STERLING/HART HAVE THE TOP-OF-THE-LINE GEAR THEY NEED TO EVEN THE ODDS, AND AS EZREN HART SAID HERSELF AT THE BRR BANQUET, THEY'RE HERE TO WIN. I DON'T KNOW ABOUT YOU, MY BELROYS, BUT I'M READY TO WITNESS HISTORY THIS WEEK.

WHILE WE'RE WAITING FOR THE STARTING GUN THOUGH, IF YOU MISSED OUT ON THE TOPSUIT FUNDRAISING SPRINT YESTERDAY AND WANT TO GET IN ON THE ACTION, EZREN'S OFFICIAL "TEAL SKIES FOR BELETHEA" FUND IS STILL OPEN. IF YOU WANT TO GIVE IT A BOOST AND HELP SAVE OUR TERRAFORMING RESEARCH FROM CERTAIN DEATH, WE APPRECIATE EACH AND EVERY CRED.

WITH THAT OBLIGATORY BUZZKILL OUT OF THE WAY, ONLY T-MINUS SIXTY-THREE MINUTES UNTIL THE RACE OF THE YEAR STARTS, AND I'M COUNTING DOWN EVERY SECOND! DON'T BLINK, KIN, WE'LL BE FOLLOWING EACH STEP RIGHT HERE UNTIL STERLING/HART CROSSES THAT FINISH LINE IN THE HEART OF THE CHURN BELT.

AND YOU KNOW *THEY'RE GOING TO DO IT FIRST.*

Micah smiled to herself as the holo faded, and the comments poured in. Still high on the success of the topsuit effort, everything seemed possible. And even though Micah had barely closed her eyes in the last two days, the thought of sleep was nothing but ridiculous.

Because after a whole year of waiting, the BRR was *happening*.

With another excited squeak, she bounced around the room, projecting a half dozen holos of starting line coverage across the walls. Her cheeks already ached from smiling as she rapid-fired responses to BRR fans and fellow hologgers, all of them thrilling in their shared anticipation.

Thank the suns Dr. Lutz had given her the week off for the BRR. Of course, with the outpost's impending closure, she was about to have a *lot* of weeks off. She'd barely let herself think about what she would do if Tuzuno closed. With most of the other terraforming outposts facing a similar fate, she'd probably have to go back home to Pyrrhia Station to live with her parents while she scrambled for a new job.

The thought of returning to the tiny space warren of Pyrrhia Station in utter defeat racked her shoulders with a bitter shudder. While her dorm here was small, her parents' station-sized apartment was hardly bigger, and her parents hadn't exactly been supportive when she'd struck out from Pyrrhia anyway. As station engineers, they were almost certainly rooting for terraforming to fail so the Beletheans were forced back to the stars, and she wasn't sure if she could stomach their smug glee if she returned home.

Her hands tightened into fists, her lightning-bolt-adorned fingernails digging into her palms.

Nope. It wasn't happening.

Because Sterling/Hart would win, and they would change everything.

Energized with fresh resolve, she pivoted to start a live stream when a priority comment chimed in her VSoc parlor.

The Royaler Review: Please keep in mind, as a rookie team, Sterling/Hart's odds are still fifty to one. Drama does not equate to performance, and they've had a hastily promoted VSoc manager as an interim coach for the last year. Which means that Ezren Hart has *never* had a certified coach, and to date, Belethea's only top-ten finish was exactly forty-eight years ago. Not to mention, every team that has *ever* won has had a second double as protection at the starting line, which we all know Belethea does not have.

Micah stopped her joyful bouncing, and her eyes narrowed. "That mother-fodder."

Any comment from VSoc accounts with over a certain level of cred got a priority label and floated to the top of the hololog until someone with more cred commented. Though she'd certainly had a few fritzes with *The Royaler Review* before and was well familiar with their complete disdain for Team Belethea, she wasn't going to let them ruin the BRR start with their ugly comment on her hype post.

Micah: With all due respect, RR, odds don't equate to heart. Something all of my Belroy boys and babes know, but you, my soulless net leech, do not.

Still internally fuming, she jumped to the *Review*'s VSoc parlor, which was filled with race-day interviews, commentary, and footage from the starting line. Jealousy twisted her gut as the fans screamed in the massive spectator dome outside of Petraskis. She would've given her left kidney to be there, but Dr. Lutz could barely afford to pay her as it was, and even though she'd officially graduated with her terraforming engineering degree a few months ago, she'd be paying off her tuition for another three years.

And yet, somehow, *The Royaler Review* had four people there in the thick of everything. Her lips tightened as she clicked to read their hololog bio, looking for more ammunition she could throw in their troll face.

As with the majority of Beletheans, the RR founders hadn't been born on Belethea, but had moved there to start their hololog only a few years ago. Micah's lip curled. What a shaft move to set up their miserable operation on Belethea only to spout chaff about their team. Still... they'd risen so much in that time. Though Micah's following had skyrocketed along with Ezren's own trajectory, she was nowhere near the RR's credibility and wider brand recognition. At the end of the day, the BRR was her passion, but not her job, and the RR didn't have that distinction.

Even if they were a bunch of fritzers.

The Royaler Review: When you have measurable stats on "heart," feel free to contact us.

Micah wrinkled her nose. While still annoying, the comment was at least preferable to the last one they'd left, and... when Sterling/Hart did win, the poetic justice of replying to this comment would be so fodding crisp.

Leaving it unanswered, she instead sent a message out to all of Tuzuno Outpost.

Micah: Don't forget the BRR starting-line party in the atrium!

A flurry of excited replies flew into her goggs... but of course it was the one sour one that stood out.

Beatrice: I've told you a million times to leave me off of your idiotic mass messages. Why don't you put your energy to good use for once instead of wasting your time obsessing over some stupid sporting event and your brain-rotting hololog.

Micah let out a tense breath through her cheeks, steam practically hissing from her ears as she snapped back.

Micah: Okay, no one let Beatrice in. Her fun allergy might be lethal.

She probably shouldn't have sent it, but... oh well. A smug, bitter-tasting grin tilted Micah's lips. Although most everyone in Tuzuno had gotten behind Sterling/Hart and the funding effort to raise creds for high-end topsuits, the lab's finance manager had been downright appalled that Micah had "put mass entertainment over the jobs and well-being of everyone in Tuzuno."

While Micah had tried to explain the ties between Sterling/Hart's performance and the lab's fundraising efforts, she couldn't deny the guilt that twinged her gut. After all, she'd spent nearly every spare moment outside her day job trying to promote Ezren and Foster through her hololog. Hours upon hours had gone into tweaking her brand for optimal performance and presenting statistically-proven narrative themes paired with perfect holos for maximum impact.

If she'd used that time and energy to help Tuzuno instead, maybe they wouldn't be facing mass eviction. Maybe she wouldn't have a string of failed relationships that couldn't survive outside of VSoc's cultivated sphere. Or the long string of insulting messages and dismissive sneers that made it no secret what the world thought of fangirls like her: mindless spongers, opportunistic groupies, groveling wannabes...

She shook her head, defiance heating her skin all over again. No, she *wasn't* wasting her time. This *meant* something. Not just for her best friend, but for the system as a whole. The BRR was the linchpin that brought them all together, and she refused to let someone steal her joy. Setting her jaw, she tapped out another response. After all, if everyone was getting fired next week, she might as well burn this bridge while she could.

Micah: And don't worry, when Ezren wins and saves this outpost, I'll remember to leave you off the invite list for our celebration.

This was Belethea's moment, and if they believed hard enough, she knew Ezren and Foster would feel it all the way from the starting line. Together, they could change everything. She'd known it since she'd first seen Ezren and Foster terra-sailing through the storm in the Belethea open tryout.

They were a legend in the making.

Micah marched out into the corridor on her way to the atrium, her smile faltering at the holopro shutdown notice circling the wall.

Sterling/Hart *had to be* a legend.

Because she'd put her *everything* into this, and if they weren't a legend, then she'd be just another heartbroken, useless fangirl with no idea what to do next.

MICAH'S INTO THE CHURN SERIES
TIMELINE

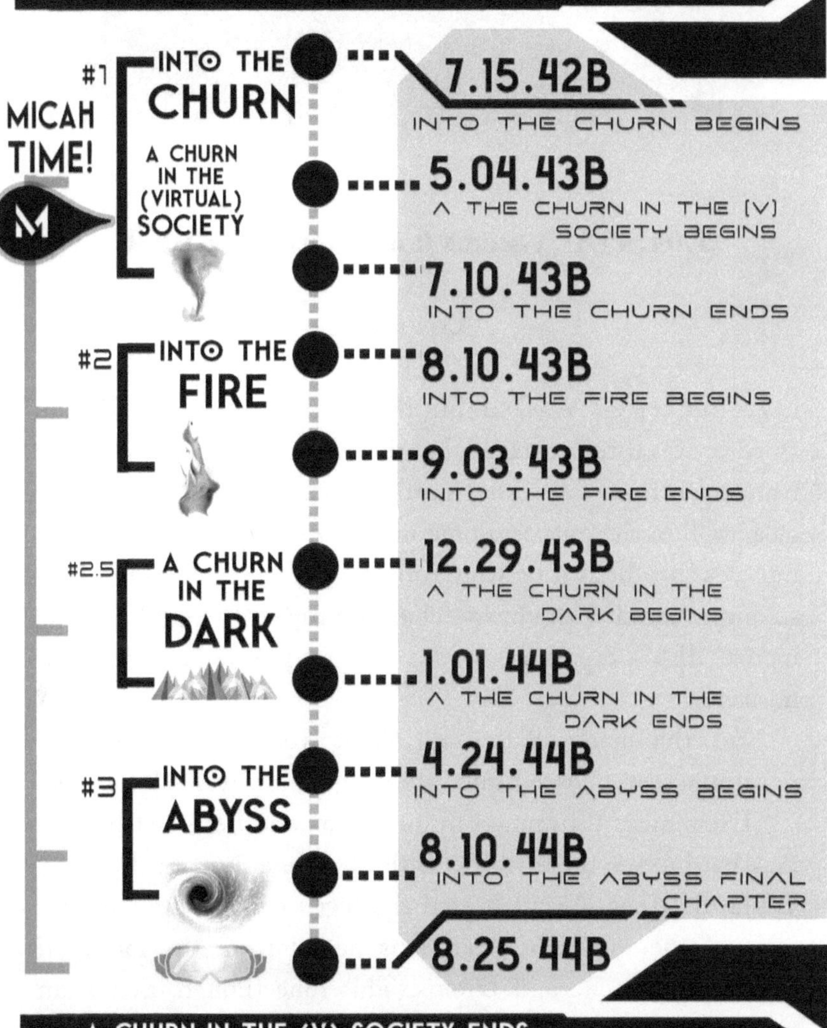

5.04.43B: T-MINUS 0 DAYS UNTIL THE BRR

LOWELL

LOWELL HAD WATCHED the start of every Race Royale since he was three years old, but this was the first time he'd ever watched it from the *actual* starting line. He stood behind the clear wall of the outpost dome in a small, empty press box, his muscles as tight as if he were running himself. Behind him, the stadium roared with cheers while the royalers strode onto the mauve dirt—preparing to race out to the lightning-strafed horizon.

Yes, this made all the late nights worth it. The years of nonstop research, travel, and interviews. They were all for this.

Excitement thrummed through him, and he didn't have to look hard to see there was something different about this year. While Belethea always hosted the biggest race of the season, most of the intensely rabid fans hailed from the moneyed planets of Obrone and Dreitis. This time though, Belethean teal competed for footing in the stands among Casolla's rainbow of other colors.

Joss, the second of the Coppen siblings, burst into the room and squeezed his shoulders. "There's still time to get your bets in. Who's it going to be this year?"

"Don't let Roland hear you say that." Lowell turned to gaze out the clear dome at the wicked storm lancing the mountains in the distance. "*The Royaler Review*'s whole brand is an unbiased fact source, and this is the *first* year we've been big enough to merit an invite."

"Suns." Joss rolled his eyes, pushing his curly brown pompadour away from his forehead. "People want opinions—*scandal*—they want to get heated and fight for their team's honor in the comments. We should just accept Obrone's offer to go exclusive and rake in the creds."

"Then start your own hololog." Lowell shook his head, only half-listening to Joss's response while he monitored *The Royaler Review* mentions on VSoc. As the notifications popped up in his feed, an algorithm assigned each mention to him or one of his siblings based on keywords. Between the four of them, each was responsible for a quarter of the total fifty teams here, with an even distribution of skill between their allotments.

Lowell, however, also had a secondary algorithm he was working on that flagged their mentions in regard to the political and financial aspects of the race: endorsements, funding, advertising, terranium investment... the list went on. While he and his siblings had yet to cover anything other than the race itself, now that they'd finally gotten a foothold of respectability in the hologger world, it was the perfect time to expand.

But first, he had to convince Roland—his oldest brother and the owner of *The Royaler Review*.

Lowell's brows furrowed as a mention popped up on a hololog run by a familiar-looking girl with teal pigtails. "Suns, Joss, are you harassing the Belethean team again? You're supposed to be covering them fairly just like the rest of the teams."

"What do you mean harassing? I ask them hard-hitting questions just like everyone else." Joss sniffed, crossing his arms.

"She called us a soulless net leech. That's not exactly good for PR."

"Sure it is, all press is good press." Joss's holo glowed from his orange goggs, an indignant tilt to his chin. "Besides, they wouldn't give me an interview today."

"That's because you're always obnoxious." Lowell ran a hand through his tangle of curls. "Chaff, what are we going to do if they win and the coach won't even talk to you?"

Joss snorted and clapped a hand on his shoulder. "Please. Like Belethea would ever win."

"My money's on them," Flora—Lowell's younger sister by a scant thirteen months—said as she entered the room, and Roland balked from where he trailed behind her.

"Don't even say that, Flora. Our niche is an unbiased local source," Roland hissed through his thick brown beard. "Fan hologs are a dime a dozen. The whole reason they invited us is because we cover all the teams impartially."

Lowell gave Joss his best I-told-you-so glare, not that it had any effect at all.

"Anyway..." Flora pushed her curtain of copper hair behind her shoulders. "The race starts in three minutes. Did you all knock out your assigned interviews?"

Lowell's gaze darted again to Joss, but if he was about to fess up over the Belethean thing, he hid it well. And as much as Joss irritated him, he wasn't about to rat him out. "I got mine. Even though Sterling/Hart is all over VSoc, the bigger teams aren't really clocking them as a threat, and the smaller ones think they're too green to be relying on anything but luck."

"Which is exactly what I've been saying," Joss said. "The facts."

Roland ran a hand through his brown mane, the unruly ends just tickling his broad shoulders. "Right. Well, they're too popular to ignore, and considering that I don't see your assigned Belethea interview online, I'm guessing Coach Long rejected you again."

Joss purpled. "It's not my fault they're so fodding thin-skinned."

"I'm not saying it is," Roland said. "But with that in mind, I'm reassigning Team Belethea coverage to Lowell for now, and you can have Hydronza instead." Roland's brown eyes turned to Lowell's matching gaze. "Make sure your updates are frequent and objective and that you're engaging with the community on different issues with a *neutral* tone."

"Fine by me." Joss turned toward the royalers milling on the starting line outside the glass window, the picture of nonchalance. "Who wants to cover a losing team that got here by divine intervention anyway?"

"Well, if they end up winning, you're going to feel like the biggest half-brain in Casolla, and our whole brand that got us this far is going to be shafted," Roland said. "We've finally risen up on this platform, and we're not going to change it now."

"Which is why we'll never be rich." Joss sighed, unfazed by his censure. "If we're not going to accept any of the exclusive team offers, at least assign Lowell a gossip column already."

Lowell's gut burned, but he forced his countenance to remain impassive. Reacting would only encourage him. "I'm all for expanding. But since you brought it up, why don't you do the gossip column, and let me and Flora take the political and financial angles of the race? Growing our expertise beyond strictly royale coverage could increase our reach and VSoc cred exponentially."

"I agree with Lowell," Flora said, and Lowell could almost see the usual sibling battle lines being drawn. The two youngest Coppens against Joss with Roland as the referee. Even now that they were all in their twenties, the sibling dynamics remained unchanged. "If we want to be a serious hololog, we have to cover serious topics," Flora added.

"Boring." Joss feigned a yawn. "Gossip sells. And if you two won't do it, then I know a girl we can hire on."

Lowell opened his mouth to snap back when Roland held up a hand. "Just stop, you three. We'll see what happens at the finish line. For now can we just enjoy the start?"

And still, Joss's mouth opened yet again. "Well—"

"That means *shut up*, Joss," Flora said just as someone popped their head into the room and beckoned to Roland. Joss, being the unfailingly nosy snoop that he was, tagged along, and Lowell took advantage of the moment to put space between him and his brother.

While on some level, he was sure he loved Joss, today he was about to drive him fritzing insane. He checked on that stupid comment Joss had left on the Belroy girl's page and read her blistering response before typing out a more moderate reply.

The Royaler Review: When you have measurable stats on "heart," feel free to contact us.

That was fair, he reasoned. The exact factual tone they were going for. His attention strayed to the official *Royaler Review* holos and he projected them onto the wall to one side. All four of the feeds focused on the top-favored teams. On a hunch, he diverted his focus to the Belethea team instead. The broad figure of Sterling pressed his helmet against Hart's smaller form, their new Gen XLII suits glowing amid the dark navy clouds.

His chest warmed at the obvious connection flowing

between them. Though he didn't regret his 24/7 dedication to *The Royaler Review*, especially when it had gotten them this far, it didn't stop him from missing the things he'd given up along the way. It was frankly amazing that Sterling/Hart's relationship seemed to make them stronger instead of detracting from the intense focus the BRR demanded. Perhaps that explained the ferocity of their new fanbase as well.

While Lowell didn't have a favorite team by any means, the Beletheans' underdog story had been blasted all over Casolla in the last few weeks—a VSoc campaign that honestly impressed him and certainly one he'd need to report on.

He tried to move to the Belethean coach's account, but apparently she'd blocked *The Royaler Review*. Ouch. Well that certainly was a complication.

He returned to the Belroy hologger's feed—Micah Belanger, her name was. The fundraiser for the suits had actually stemmed from her account, and even if she was sniping at them, at least comms were still open. If he needed to smooth over this relationship in the name of interviews and insider information, she would be their most accessible source.

Even if the Beletheans lost as badly as Joss predicted, they deserved to have their story told just like every other team here—another reason they'd started *The Royaler Review*. While they weren't the biggest or most lucrative hololog in the business, they were slowly climbing the ladder of respectability. In a world where everyone was always shouting the most outrageous thing they could come up with just to be heard, they were the steady voice people could depend on.

The next half hour ticked away before the doubles finally tensed for the starting gun. Inside the press box, Lowell and his siblings stood shoulder to shoulder, their squabbles forgotten as they looked on in awe. Joss wrapped his arms around Roland and Flora, and Flora linked her elbow with Lowell's, a grin shared between them that could weather any storm. The stadium fell into a deathly quiet in anticipation of the starting gun, the tension of his siblings singing through them just as it had for every start for as long as he could remember.

And Lowell realized that if Roland and Flora actually asked him to do the stupid relationship column, of course he would do it. Because as much as he loved the race, and the hololog they'd built around it, he'd do anything for his siblings. For the hololog they'd built together.

The gun went off, and the royalers rocketed forward, impossibly fast in their strength-enhancing topsuits. Lowell's pulse spiked with them as they crashed together in a series of scraps, and the four *Royaler Review* cams followed close behind. He and his siblings mentally dictated a running commentary for each one while their linked arms fell to their sides.

The Royaler Review: The Belethean underdogs, Sterling/Hart have taken an early lead, the advantage of their new Gen XLII suits certainly paying off in this leg of the race.

Joss: Mostly because no one else is taking them seriously. Why are we wasting a stream on them?

Flora: Wake up. They're literally the home team, and they've got an early lead.

Roland: Stop fighting and focus on your commentary. We need to get it right or this may be the last time we're invited to the starting line.

Lowell: I know the brand. I've got it.

Roland smiled at him, ruffling Lowell's hair with all the pride of his five years of seniority. "I know you do."

Joss cocked an annoyed eyebrow in their direction, but for once, said nothing, and Lowell turned his back to him.

He could do this.

Because *The Royaler Review* was their whole life. And if they didn't have their shared love of the BRR to keep them together, what did they have?

He popped into the Micah girl's feed one more time, but she'd never responded to his last comment. He wasn't sure if that was a good sign or a bad one but... A frown etched into his jaw and his attention skewed to Sterling/Hart hurtling up the slope, currently in third place.

Either way, he had a feeling it was certainly going to be a complication.

MICAH'S INTO THE CHURN SERIES TIMELINE

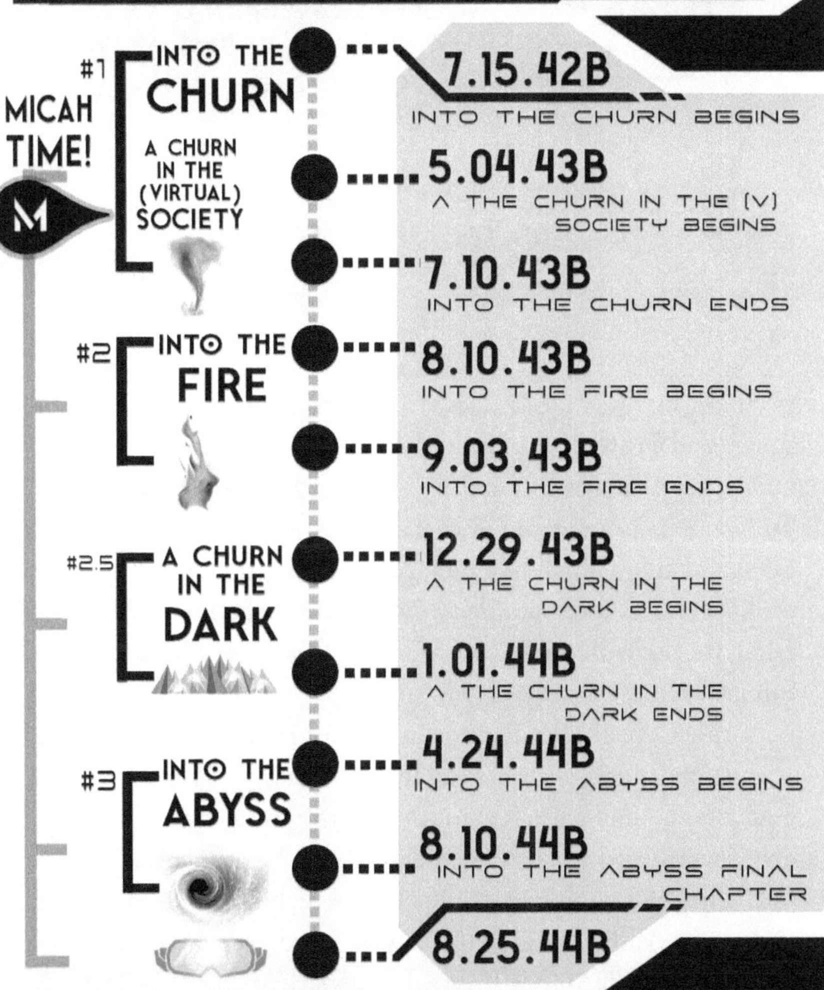

5.08.43B: BRR Day 5

Micah

WHEN THE WORD "DISPUTED" appeared in front of Ezren and Foster's names, Micah screamed right there in the middle of Tuzuno's verdant atrium garden. Around her, Tuzuno's residents erupted in their own questions and disbelief under the huge finish-line holo projected on the dome's curved wall. Tables of food and drinks stood untouched as if the gathering was still deciding on whether this was a victory or a commiseration party.

Beside Micah, Dr. Evangeline Hart's brow scrunched in an expression much like her daughter, Ezren's. "Wait, I don't understand. The rules say both royalers have to cross the finish line, and Ezren and Foster came in before the other girl."

"They're saying something about a technicality," Sam Hart said while Waffle rolled in the lush grass beside where he sat on the lawn. "But second is still really good, right?"

"No! They deserved to win!" Micah shrieked, jumping up and down as the indignant rage threatened to burn through her skin. "If they think we're just going to accept that shaft lying down they've got another thing coming. I absolutely refuse to let them take this away from us. We'll mobilize the Belroy army to fight this injus—"

Then, right there on the official BRR holo, Foster Sterling got down on one knee, and Micah screamed all over again. A shocked silence fell over Tuzuno's atrium as they listened, rapt, along with the rest of Casolla.

"Ezren Hart, would you..." Foster started, earnest anxiety rippling over his handsome face, "tell them who murdered Genevieve Navarro?"

A collective gasp ran through the crowd, and Micah could've sworn her pulse stopped, but no one dared speak as Ezren unfolded Calderon's role in both Genevieve's murder and their own sabotage. Micah's jaw hung ajar, frozen in shock while Calderon fled the stadium along with Talmadge/Brook, leaving a trail of guilt behind.

But even as hologgers swarmed Sterling/Hart for interviews, that stubborn "disputed" disclaimer never disappeared from the rightful champions. As Evangeline and Sam broke into relieved smiles and the rest of the dome fell into a din of excited chatter, Micah finally forced herself into action. Mind racing, she ducked into a deserted corridor, a sleepy, small-town holo coating the walls and her hovercam trailing behind her. The situation was too complicated for her to strategize live, but she couldn't leave it unaddressed.

"Well, Belroy boys and babes, I think we can say without a doubt we just witnessed the wildest BRR finish in history. I'm sure you can tell I'm just as shocked by the drama as you are, but I think I speak for everyone when I say I'm glad Sterling/Hart survived their trials, and I, for one, will not rest until they are rightfully acknowledged as the BRR champions." She paused to take a breath and forced her expression into a VSocapproved grin. "And let's not forget, my Belroys, that would never have been possible without every cred of support we got them for those last-minute topsuits. This was truly a team effort, and I couldn't think of a happier ending. Now to celebrate!"

With another squeal, Micah ended the recording, and her smile abruptly fell. She had so much to do, and if they wanted to influence the delicate narrative spinning through VSoc, time was of the essence. But first she needed some advice. Head still spinning with a flux of emotions, she reached out to Jabari, a Petraskis-based BRR hologger she'd known for a few years now. Conveniently, he also happened to be dating one half of the Amaral/Amaral doubles team Micah was not-so-subtly trying to recruit for Belethea next season.

A holo of Jabari's head and shoulders popped up in front of her. Teal swirls accented his bowler hat where his bronze goggs strapped around it, and a teal ascot wrapped around his high white collar before tucking into his black vest. The glow of a dozen holos lit his dark brown skin with a golden sheen while his gaze swiveled everywhere but at her.

"Tell me you have the inside juice on what's going on right now," Jabari said.

"I know as much as you." Micah let herself lean against the wall, her legs wobbly after averaging four hours of sleep for the last week. "But I'm worried about how the hologgers are going to spin the story. Takes are already popping up labeling Belethea as cheaters and thieves. Some are even calling for them to be disqualified."

"I'm seeing it, but without further information, it's all just baseless rumors. Have you heard anything from the team yet?"

"Sylvia just said Ezren and Foster are pretty banged up, and they're focusing on their recovery before they address the murder attempt and Calderon's race interference." Micah could barely grasp the words she was saying, the gravity of it too much to take in.

"Murder and rigging." Jabari shook his head as his dark gaze finally latched on to hers. "Chaff, those are huge accusations. I'm sure Calderon Industries is already throwing money at hologgers to tell their side."

"Right." Anxiety and defiance surged through Micah all over again. "But we need to make sure the truth gets out." She pulled up a hololog of her trusted contacts, mentally dictating a mass message to rally Sterling/Hart's defense in the VSoc sphere. "Can you send me any hololog names, especially professional ones, that are sympathetic to Belethea's cause?"

"On it." Jabari's hands flew through the air as he rearranged his holos. "But you know... most of the hologs have a team sponsor, and with the Belethean team as the disputed champs, it seems more likely they'll use their sour grapes to paint them as a villain."

Micah stifled a groan and let herself sag to the floor of the hallway. "Okay, if not sympathetic, maybe at least neutral?"

Jabari tapped his fingers along the rim of his bowler, a carefully thoughtful expression ironing his features. "Well... there's *The Royaler Review*."

Micah reared back as if the very notion had slapped her. "They're not neutral! They've never said a single nice word about the Belethean team."

"Yeah... they can be a bit snarky, but they're one of the few that cover Belethea, and they're local to Petraskis too." Jabari cocked his head with a shrug. "I've even met the founder, Roland Coppen. He seems pretty crisp."

Wiping a hand across her face, Micah pulled up the comment that had been marring her feed for the last five days.

The Royaler Review: When you have measurable stats on "heart," feel free to contact us.

Even if it wasn't outright hostile, there was a definite tone, and she'd been so looking forward to throwing it back in RR's face. Instead, she let out a long sigh. "Okay, like I'm five, what exactly are you saying, Jabari?"

"I'm saying, Micah..." Jabari flashed her an almost apologetic smile that had won over his rapidly growing fanbase. "It'd be nice to have them on our side."

"Noooo." Micah petulantly kicked her feet against the corridor's metal floor as if she were, indeed, five. "They suck the fun out of everything. They have no passion, Jabari. They're like a bland blender of stats and the obvious. And the only time they have even the teensiest bit of flair is when they're taking cheap snark-shots at us."

"I know." Jabari's attention flicked back to his holos. "But if you want to have more of an impact, you have to expand your influence beyond the fans."

"But I'm just a fangirl, Jabari, that's *literally* where my influence lies." Hateful messages about lawyers, system-wide repercussions, and accusations of her spreading parasocial lies dinged into Micah's goggs, and cold doubt oozed through her veins. This was all feeling too big for her.

"You are a fangirl, Micah, but you're also one of the best advocates the Belethea team has. If you want to win here, you'll need to use every avenue and advantage open to you, even the ones you don't like. Sometimes work is fun, but sometimes work is work."

"But... it'll have to be flawless..." Micah pressed her shaking hands to her flushed cheeks, her mind already whirling with everything that needed to be done. She could leave no cracks for further criticism or her whole brand could fall apart, and with Sterling/Hart in such a precarious position, she could very well pull them down with her.

"It doesn't have to be flawless, it just has to be done." Jabari shot her a steady glance that made him seem much older than his eighteen years. "If you care about it, you'll do it. So I guess you just have to ask yourself—how much do you care?"

"More than anyone!" Micah shouted, the words echoing in the corridor. She peeked over her shoulder, but everyone in the atrium was still too busy celebrating to notice she was missing. "Okay, well, *maybe* not more than Ezren or Foster," she amended in a reasonable volume. "But honestly it's a toss-up."

"Then you'd better get to work." Jabari flashed her an encouraging smile. "I'll do what I can from here, but call me when you have more."

"Will do. And..." She leaned in with a conspiratorial whisper. "Don't forget to let your girlfriend know that Belethea would love to have her." And *you*, she mentally added. Considering she had a day job to attend to, she did reasonably well as a Belethea VSoc hologger army of one, but... an army of two would certainly be an upgrade.

Jabari let out a low chuckle. "I'll let Kit and Dean know."

"Thanks, Jabari." With that, Micah ended the call, letting her head roll back with a slow exhale. As much as she wanted to be celebrating with the others right now, she, as the general of Belethea's VSoc fanbase, was now in a race to control the message. These were the most crucial moments, and she couldn't waste them.

Taking a fortifying breath, Micah projected *The Royaler Review*'s hololog in front of her. To her surprise, they'd been following Ezren and Foster from the starting line. While they didn't have an extensive feature on them, their status on the situation encompassed direct quotes from Ezren, Foster, and Calderon with a note that more details would be shared as they were accumulated.

Boring, yes. But Jabari was right, that was why they were respected as an impartial source. Which meant, if they were to report Ezren and Foster's story… or better… give a detailed review of the regulations that proved they were indeed the true winner, more people would give them credence than a raving fangirl of admittedly extreme bias like herself.

Her lips twisted as she dove into their background. After all, she had to consider them an enemy until proven otherwise. With the stakes as high as they were, she couldn't afford to underestimate them.

A family-run business, *The Royaler Review* consisted of four siblings: Roland, 29; Joss, 26; Lowell, 24; and Flora, 23. Roland sported a mane of curly brown hair, an impressively wild beard, and an easy expression while Joss paired a sleek pompadour with a model's conceited air. The younger two had dark auburn hair with Flora's luxurious waves flowing to her waist, and Lowell's moppish curls falling across his brow. Their matching brown eyes and creamy complexions marked them clearly as a sibling set, but she had to admit they were an attractive bunch—something she was sure had helped them in the VSoc sphere.

Apparently they were each assigned different teams in their Race Royale coverage, and it looked like Joss had been the one sniping at Team Belethea. Which she probably could've guessed since he practically had asschaff scrolled across his pompous face.

Opening his stupid comment on her VSoc, she thought out a private message that was not at all the publicly humiliating response she really wanted to make.

MICAH: I SINCERELY HOPE AS FELLOW BELETHEANS, WE'LL BE ABLE TO PUT ASIDE OUR DIFFERENCES TO REPORT ON THIS SITUATION FAIRLY IN ORDER TO TRUTHFULLY INFORM THE PEOPLE OF CASOLLA OF THE HISTORICAL EVENT THAT HAS TAKEN PLACE TODAY.

There. She was just giving herself a moment to gloat about taking the high road when a response chimed in her goggs.

The Royaler Review: Even when you find our commentary unfavorable, we are and have always been an unbiased news source. We have and will continue to do our jobs as such. However, we applaud your efforts as a team-affiliated personal hololog to promote truth over drama in this situation.

Micah seethed, her fury escaping in an enraged squeak as she closed out of the hololog with a snap of her hand. As if *she* was the one causing trouble and spreading drama? She let out a muted scream before slamming her teeth together with a click. Forget *The Royaler Review* and their snobbery. While they might be a respected professional hololog, it was clear they didn't respect the fans and especially not *her*. Leaping to her feet, she turned back toward the atrium. She could figure this out with the other true BRR enthusiasts who actually cared about the integrity of the race.

Respect be shafted. After all, she'd gotten this far without it.

But even as the thought crossed her mind, the comments poured into her hololog, hate practically radiating through her goggs.

And she could not ignore the sharp teeth of doubt biting into her.

MICAH'S INTO THE CHURN SERIES TIMELINE

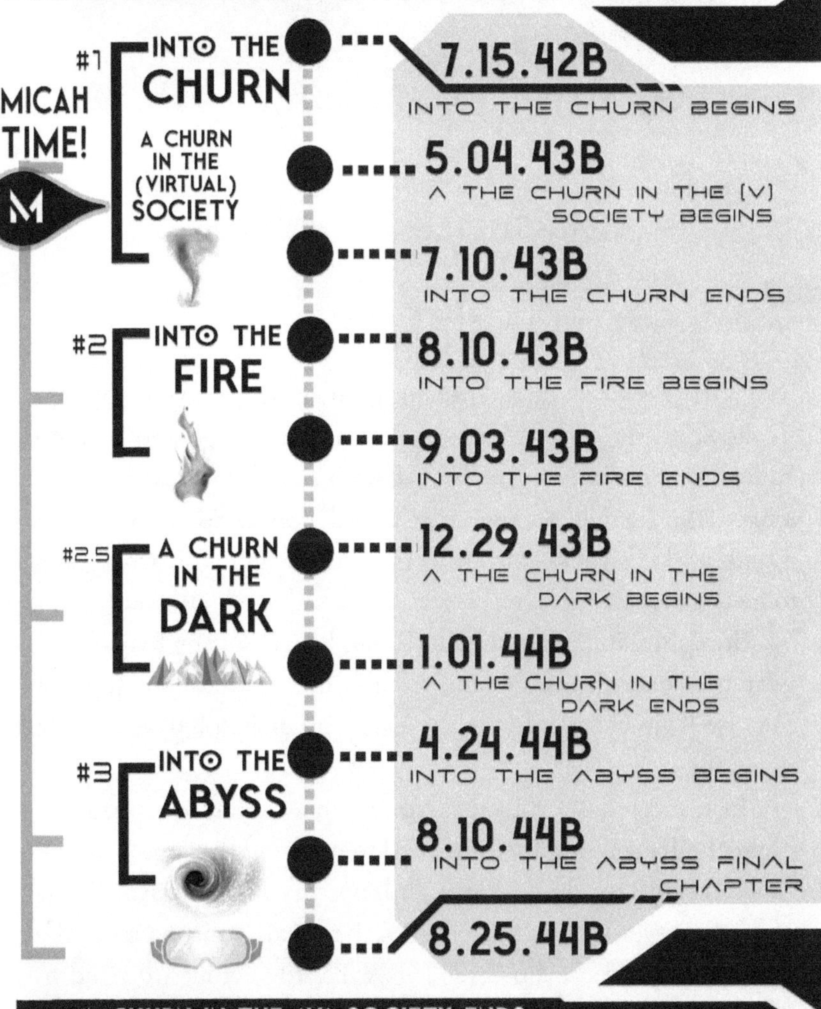

5.08.43B: Day 5 of the BRR

Lowell

IN THE SWARM of the finishing line dome, Lowell watched in shock as the authorities took Lucian Talmadge and Celesta Brook into custody. The four Coppen siblings stood frozen amidst the turmoil of the crowd, and Lowell realized in that moment, the biggest story to come out of the day wasn't going to be the race itself.

Straightening, he turned to Roland, steel setting his jaw. "If we don't cover the other political and financial ramifications of this, we'll be overshadowed by every other hololog in Casolla that does."

Joss snorted. "And don't forget that ridiculous proposal. Holy chaff, even our ancestors had to cringe at that one."

"Oh, shut up, Joss," Flora said, her sharp eyes grave. "Now more than ever before, this is so much more than just a race. We can't play it safe because it's times like these that we need to speak up the most."

The seconds ticked by, and Roland only stood there,

conflict waging in his eyes. Just when Lowell thought he was about to turn them down yet again, Joss spoke up.

"They're not wrong, Roland." His expression soured as if that small admission pained him. "And if we cover both sides of the issue, we'd attract viewers from opposite ends of the spectrum without losing objectivity." His mouth tilted in a smirk. "But to be clear, I want to cover Calderon's stance."

If Lowell wasn't already maximally shocked, that would've blown his chip. Joss was actually agreeing with them? Then again, of course, he'd picked what was sure to be the prevailing viewpoint. With Joss, it always came down to VSoc cred.

Roland scrubbed a hand through his long beard, and Lowell could practically see his arguments falling away. "Okay. Fine. But we have to plan this right." Lowell and Flora exchanged a victorious smile, and even Joss had an excited gleam in his eye as they all leaned closer. Roland pointed to each of them in turn. "Joss gets Calderon's perspective; Lowell, you're covering Team Belethea's; and Flora, I want the detailed financial ramifications of all possible impacts of today." He fiddled with the goggs around his neck. "I'll stick with the racing coverage, but I want to let you know, we're just doing this on a trial basis for the offseason. If it doesn't work out, we're back to our tried-and-true BRR niche on opening day. This is your one chance."

Opportunity flew through Lowell's veins on fluttering wings, and he broke into a smile. "Thanks, Roland. We'll make it count."

Then Roland shooed them away with a wave. "All right, now get out of here. We've got to move fast if we want to get ahead of this."

Needing no more encouragement, Joss ran toward Talmadge while Flora raced toward the ambassadors' viewing boxes, and Roland headed back to the finish line where Dreitis was taking third.

Lowell shouldered through the mass of hologgers toward the trainers shepherding the limping Sterling/Hart to the recovery room with Lowell's jacket around Hart's shoulders. When he'd seen her on the ground hurting and nearly naked under the eyes of a thousand hovercams, it was the least he could offer.

Even now, empathy and awe echoed through him as he watched Sterling, his face still blood-streaked and bruised, lift Hart into his arms and follow behind a particularly bulky looking security guard. At that moment, Lowell understood the hype. But what had really happened out there? And more importantly, with multiple stories muddying the waters, how could he find out?

He projected a handful of holos in front of him, *The Royaler Review*'s inbox blowing up with demands. There were messages from Obrone and Dreitis offering an incentive if they reported that the Beletheans had cheated. Another from Calderon Industries dangling their own exclusive interviews—which explained Joss's sudden amenability. Several teams were asking them to report that both Sterling/Hart and Brook/Talmadge should be disqualified.

But his messages to Coach Sylvia Long, Team Belethea's VSoc manager and temporary coach, had gone unread and unanswered.

Mother suns, they were in trouble.

He tugged at his tie, his collar suddenly too hot. They'd all worked their asses off to get *The Royaler Review* invited to the finish line for the first time ever. And if he screwed this up, the plummet into obscurity was only one wrong step away.

His skin itching with anxiety, he sent a hasty message to his sister.

Lowell: I'm going to shaft this up.

Flora: No, you're not. You're going to do the work, and we're going to pull this off.

Lowell: But Team Belethea has blocked us. How am I supposed to find the truth without direct interviews?

Flora: Get creative and do it well. You're a better reporter than Joss, but he's going to have the masses on his side. Just because Belethea won doesn't mean they're not the underdog here. It's up to you to make sure they get justice. That's what we're all about, and you care more about this than he does. You can do this.

Lowell took a deep breath. Even though his sister was younger than him, she always had a knack for saying exactly what he needed to hear. It was what made her the best reporter on *The Royaler Review*, and if they didn't expand, it was only a matter of time before she accepted a better opportunity. And he really couldn't imagine *The Royaler Review* without all four of them in it.

Lowell: Okay, I'll try.

Flora: That's why you're my favorite. Can't wait to see what you get.

Closing out the comms from his goggs, he tugged his tie loose before unfastening the restrictive buttons of his collar. He ducked into an empty press breakroom and threw his tie onto one of the many armchairs that punctuated the space. Pacing back and forth, he considered the Belroy girl's hololog where only twenty minutes ago he'd posted a defensive reaction about not taking sides. *Great.* Grimacing, he rolled up his shirt sleeves while he weighed his options.

If they wanted to tell this story right, he absolutely had to tell Belethea's side of it. He brought up their coverage of the finish again, Ezren's screams from the holo as her topsuit had obviously malfunctioned. But it was only when he rewatched Calderon claiming innocence and fleeing the scene that he realized that he didn't just want to tell Belethea's side, he genuinely wanted to get to the bottom of the truth. Because if what Sterling/Hart claimed was correct, then Calderon had to be held accountable.

And... he swiped through Micah Belanger's past holos of Ezren and Foster. There was more here than he'd seen in any one spot, and they were all original media. He vaguely remembered a friend of Hart's coming to her defense in some sort of drama when she first tried out for Belethea's BRR team. If Micah had known Ezren before fame, that explained the close connection and also meant that she'd probably get the real juice before anyone else.

Which left him no choice but to try to bridge the divide... A divide that he was partially responsible for. *Shaaffft.* With a resigned huff, he thought out the message.

The Royaler Review: I've come to understand that you have a close relationship with the BRR team, and I'd like to inquire if you'd be open to an offline interview in the name of getting to the truth of the situation.

There. Lowell nodded to himself as he sank into one of the armchairs. That sounded good. Professional... but not unfriendly. If she didn't respond though, what would he do then? He already knew that neither Foster nor Ezren answered interview requests that didn't go through their coach so—

He was saved from further waffling as his goggs beeped.

Micah: Only if you agree to portray the Belethea team in a favorable light.

The Royaler Review: *The Royaler Review* is committed to covering all sides of the issue. My job is telling Belethea's story, but that doesn't mean we're going to be biased in your favor.

Micah: Interesting. Will you at least promise to have an open mind?

The Royaler Review: I always have an open mind.

Micah: That is neither an answer nor a promise.

The Royaler Review: Fine, I promise to have an open mind.

Micah: My, my, that was easier than I thought. Maybe we can work together after all.

The Royaler Review: Are you going to be able to be professional about this?

Micah: I'm going to be authentic. Isn't that what you really want?

The Royaler Review: I just want to know the truth.

Micah: All right then, Joss. Interrogate me. I'm not scared of you.

The Royaler Review: Joss is my brother. This is Lowell, and it looks like you're livestreaming a BRR victory party right now.

Micah: Of course I am. Ezren and Foster are obviously the winners. You're reporting that, right?!?!?! You'd better be reporting that.

The Royaler Review: The official statement is that it's disputed.

Micah: Which is obviously a load of fodding shaft.

The Royaler Review: How do you know?

Micah: Um, because I saw them come across the finish line with my *eyeballs*. Unless you're saying the feed is fake. In which case, I have all kinds of questions, you fritzing conspiracy chaffer.

The Royaler Review: Whoa, chill your chip, fangirl. I'm not saying that. Officials are reporting they have to finish with their topsuits.

Micah: And I'm messaging with BRR historians at this moment to see if a royaler has ever finished without their gear in the past and if that affected their official finisher designation. Spoiler, I bet the answer's no. So you can go ahead and throw your next excuse at me. I'm ready for you.

The Royaler Review: And by BRR historians, you mean the Belethean fans? I can see them discussing it on your page.

Micah: No one knows the BRR better than them.

The Royaler Review: I think the officials would disagree.

Micah: Okay then, bring them to BRR trivia night, and we'll settle it once and for all.

The Royaler Review: Look, just... if they can find evidence of a case, let me know so I can verify. What do you know about the budding Calderon allegations?

Micah: Tsk, tsk, Viewboy, you're asking the wrong questions. The only people who know more than us right now are Foster and Ezren. Go interview them.

The Royaler Review: It's Lowell. And I can't... Coach Long hasn't responded to a message from us in six months.

Micah: Ha! Serves you right! You reported that Genevieve Navarro's death was an *accident*. Ouch. That's not going to age well.

The Royaler Review: No, we reported that the officials deemed her death an accident.

Micah: Right. I'm sure her family will lovvvvveee that.

The Royaler Review: We never said it wasn't a tragedy.

Micah: Mother suns, you're going to drive me sparking insane. Listen close, you said you want the truth. But there's a difference between what the officials say and the truth.

The Royaler Review: And that's why I'm interviewing you.

Micah: Fine, then you can quote me here. I know Ezren Hart better than almost anyone, and she wouldn't know how to lie to save her life. If she says Calderon killed Genevieve Navarro then I believe her. I always had my creds on Lucian Talmadge, so it doesn't surprise me that he's involved, and it would be a pretty big coincidence if this wasn't connected to Grady/Guns's near-death "accident" as well.

The Royaler Review: That sounds like a fan conspiracy theory.

Micah: Oh, okay, so you're going to be conceited about this too? Let me just remind you that you came to *me* for my side. You may look down on us lowly fangirls, but I'm giving you my opinion and labeling it as such. As far as I'm concerned, the only person who's sold lies as the truth is *you*.

The words hit Lowell like a punch to the chest, the breakroom suddenly too quiet while the fans roared outside.

The Royaler Review: You're right.

Micah: Holy chaff, am I still talking to *The*

Royaler Review? Or has someone hacked into our comms?!?

The Royaler Review: But to play devil's advocate: is there any reason Sterling/Hart would want to frame Calderon?

Micah: Before they crossed that finish line, I hadn't heard his name come out of Ezren's mouth. And they seemed friendly enough at the banquet. Check out my pre-race montage; the footage is there. But let's be real, if Bex, Genevieve, and Ezren all had suit issues, that's more than just conspiracy, that's a connection, and if the corrupt code is tied to Calderon Industries too...

The Royaler Review: Circumstantial. It could've been anybody.

Micah: Okay, I'm done with you. If you only want official reports, go talk to the officials, since that worked out so well for you last time.

Lowell ran a frustrated hand over his face, ready to tear his hair out. This girl was impossible. Fighting for calm, he thought out a message to his brother.

Lowell: Roland, Team Belethea only has conjecture at this point.

Roland: That's fine. If we're going to contrast one side with the other, take their conjecture, and we'll just frame it as letting them voice their experience.

Lowell: But that isn't how we work. We report facts.

Roland: Yeah, but if you wanted to expand, Lowell, this is the gray area we have to expand into. It's either this or be silent. And you're right, to be silent is to be obsolete. So do your best to report

THEIR NARRATIVE ACCURATELY, AND LET PEOPLE DECIDE FOR THEMSELVES. JUST BECAUSE WE'RE REPORTING THEIR SIDE DOESN'T MEAN WE HAVE TO BE BIASED TOWARD IT. I TRUST YOU TO FRAME IT IN THE RIGHT WAY.

The vote of confidence both warmed Lowell and terrified him at the same time. While he knew the vote to expand had been the right move, the reality of it had him shaking under the burden of responsibility.

Lowell: Okay.

Lowell rose from the chair and paced the perimeter of the room, a holopro of a lush city park lighting the walls. *The Royaler Review* hololog indicated that three more teams had finished, but Roland was doing a good job of reporting race coverage on his own. Which meant Lowell had to do his part too. Taking a deep breath, he returned to his conversation with Micah.

The Royaler Review: Okay. I'm sorry.

Micah: Holy suns. Can I quote you on that? Wait, I need you to be more specific. Sorry for what? Don't be shy now.

The Royaler Review: I didn't mean to cast doubt on your narrative. But it may be better if we start at the beginning, and I get your full story.

Micah: Not if you're going to try to use it to discredit Sterling/Hart.

The Royaler Review: I will tell your side to the best of my ability, and you can approve it before I publish. Your story will need to be convincing though, because we will be contrasting it with Calderon's and possibly Obrone's opinion pieces as well.

Micah: And you get to publish the good side? Please tell me you at least won employee-of-the-

YEAR OR SOMETHING. CAN I REQUEST A REVIEWER WHO HASN'T ALREADY DISCOUNTED WHAT I HAVE TO SAY A DOZEN TIMES? FLORA, MAYBE?

The words stung, not because she'd insulted his ability, but because of the insinuation that she might ask for one of his siblings to report instead. Even if he harbored his own doubts on his ability to do the story justice, he refused to lose this chance.

The Royaler Review: Sorry, I'm your only option.

Micah: Siiiggghhh. Fine. But for your side, you WILL publish my proof that Sterling/Hart is the winner, and I get to make inputs on everything before you publish it regarding our story.

Lowell chewed his bottom lip... it was a big ask... but from the information Flora was already lobbing into their files, it looked like this was all going to blow up legally. With a case like this, who knew how long it could go on for—weeks, months, years... one thing was for sure, Sterling/Hart would be involved. And that kind of insider knowledge could be invaluable.

The Royaler Review: As long as you give me insights into the evolving Calderon situation over the offseason.

Micah: Deal. But it's going to take me time to collect information, and in any case, I'd like to take this moment to properly celebrate. Something I know you "*objective*" types have a hard time appreciating, but we fangirls refuse to compromise on.

The Royaler Review: That makes sense. Why don't we meet up for an interview the day after tomorrow?

Micah: Um, in person? Why? This smells like a trap.

MICAH: AND BEFORE YOU SAY ANYTHING ABOUT "*FACTS*" AGAIN, *THE ROYALER REVIEW* HAS BEEN TROLLING BELETHEA FOR THE LAST YEAR, AND NOW AT LEAST ONE COPPEN IS TRYING TO DISCREDIT MY FRIENDS AND DEFEND A MURDERER, SO YOU ARE ABSOLUTELY *NOT* ABOVE SUSPICION.

Lowell's brows knitted at her accusations—torn between the need to defend *The Royaler Review*'s honor and extricate himself from the agonizing conversation as quickly as possible. He was not the bad guy here just as much as this girl was certainly not a paragon of truth.

Which, honestly, was a problem.

The main atrium roared again as the royalers finished, each enormous achievement a victory in its own right. While Lowell wasn't exactly flush with strengths, he did happen to have a good sense about people. For example, he could tell almost without a shadow of a doubt that Calderon, Talmadge, and even Calderon's lackey, Harland, had all been hiding something in the wake of Ezren's confession. Just as he could tell how fervent Ezren had been when relating her allegations. And if he was going to tell this story, he had to know if Micah was being honest with him or if she was just trying to leech off her friend's fame for her own moment in the spotlight. After all, fan hologgers weren't exactly known for their truthfulness. Most of them would say anything to help their team.

But of course, he couldn't tell her any of that.

THE ROYALER REVIEW: I DON'T WANT TO RISK YOU LEAKING OUR CONVERSATIONS BEFORE I'M READY.

MICAH: I'M SO GLAD THIS COLLABORATION IS STARTING ON THE FIRM GROUND OF MUTUAL DISTRUST. I BET YOU'RE JUST MR. POPULAR AT PARTIES.

Warmth flooded Lowell's cheeks, and in that moment, he was grateful that she couldn't see him. This girl really didn't pull any punches, and even though she knew next to nothing about him, her words still held the sting of truth. Between keeping *The Royaler Review* afloat and trying to prevent his siblings from ripping each other's heads off, he didn't exactly have time for a social life. But he wasn't about to admit that either.

The Royaler Review: Do you want me to come to Tuzuno for the interview? Or are you in Petraskis?

Micah: Petraskis is fine.

He let out a measured breath. At least he'd be in familiar territory. With this girl's lashing barbs, he had a feeling he'd need it.

The Royaler Review: Okay then. Day after tomorrow at 1600. Dak's Pub in Petraskis.

Micah: Fiiinnneeee. I'll be there. But please try to bring a little pep. Three espresso shots should do the trick? Maybe four to be safe.

Lowell rolled his eyes. He'd officially had enough of this ridiculous fangirl.

The Royaler Review: I have a feeling you'll be bringing enough "*pep*" for the whole pub.

As Lowell stepped out of the side room and back into the fray of the BRR finish line, excited nerves tangled in his gut. Calderon and the Beletheans were on everyone's tongue, and the *Review*'s inbox was basically exploding with inquiries.

Flora was right. This was the story of the century.

And it was theirs.

He thought again of Micah with her blistering tongue and sharp eyes.

She certainly had a voice that screamed to be heard, but suns, if he wasn't careful, she was going to eat him alive.

MICAH'S **INTO THE CHURN** SERIES

TIMELINE

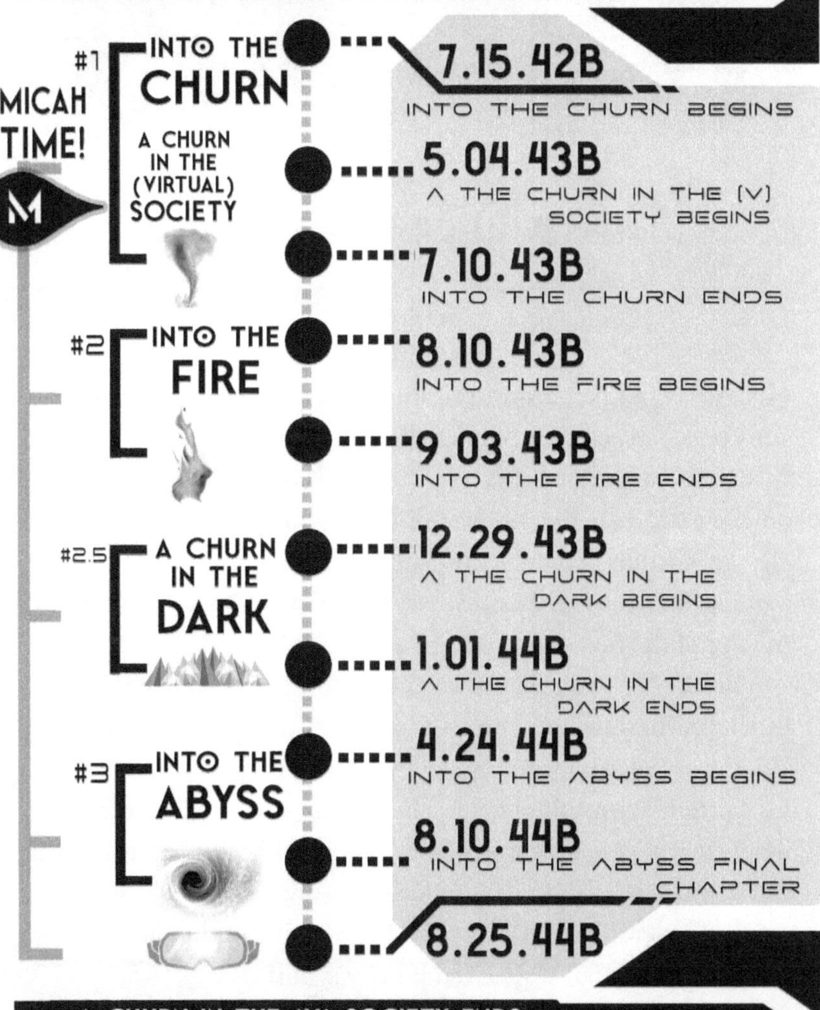

5.10.43B: Day 2 of the Offseason

Micah

MICAH WALKED into the dive bar wondering what in the suns had possessed her to do this. The dark pub had a vaguely rustic vibe with hololog ads of various local businesses blazoned on the glass partitions between booths. She was dressed casually, in a ruffled teal skirt topped with a white sweater, indigo pigtails, and rose-pink irises, but even that was enough to draw the eye of the few scattered patrons at the bar.

Before they could approach, she strode to the farthest booth in the corner where Lowell Coppen already waited for her. With his dark auburn mop spilling into his eyes, the sleeves of his button-down rolled up to his elbows, and a pair of old-fashioned metal goggs hanging from his neck, he looked every bit the stiff-necked, humorless reporter that he was.

But at least he was exactly what he appeared to be. He was less dangerous that way. Even if he was boring.

Still, with the news blowing up as it was, boring might be

just the thing they needed on their side. So while this little tête-à-tête screamed against her drama-milking fangirl instincts, she would do this. After all, it was basically her Belroy babe duty.

With a sigh, she slid into the booth across from Lowell, and his head jerked up in surprise, the dusting of freckles on his nose stark against his pale skin.

"I have to say, this wasn't the kind of place I expected a straitlaced member of *The Royaler Review* to hang out in," Micah said.

"It's for the privacy." The booth door hissed shut, and the partition around them frosted over as if to emphasize Lowell's words. "We feel the story will land better if you remain unnamed as an anonymous source."

"Uh-huh." Micah sat back and crossed her arms. Really, if he was embarrassed to be seen with a fangirl, all he had to do was say so. "Well, that works for me. If my Belroy boys and babes thought I was throwing it in with Belethea's number one hololog enemy, they'd accuse me of treason and revoke my popular card." She raised her chin with a lofty sniff. "Even I couldn't survive that one-two punch."

"I'm sure." Lowell's cheeks burned beneath his freckles, his brown eyes flashing. "And if our readers knew we were sourcing our information from the girl who falsified Ezren Hart's application to join the Belethean team, it would forever damage our credibility."

"Hey, I came clean about that!" Micah gripped the table, forcing herself not to vault across it and strangle him. While she had, in fact, tweaked Ezren's tryout application last year, she wasn't exactly proud of it. Not that she would admit it to this guy. "And now, Ezren Hart is the BRR champion, so I'd say I did the 'verse a favor."

Lowell's attention flicked to a holo menu lighting up the

scratched synwood table. "Still, I think we all know you'd say anything to get Team Belethea out of a bind."

"So what? You said you're telling both sides," Micah said as she ordered a basket of spiced fries.

"Yes, but I still want to find the truth, and I'll be reporting with that aim in mind. If I find you're lying at any point, I will cut your feature short." The center of the table opened, and a basket of fried cheese and two glasses of water appeared before them. Before she could say a word, Lowell pushed the basket and one of the cups toward her, his face still grave.

Perhaps he thought she would decline, but Micah was not the kind of girl to turn down free food... especially from the enemy. So she plucked one of the golden sticks from the basket and sank her teeth in it. "Well, the good news for you is that I'm here to find the truth too. Which is why, in exchange for my insider information on Sterling/Hart's experiences, I want access to the Belethean Council's meeting notes."

Lowell straightened, cocking his head. "Okay, but why?"

"Because I know that only certified Petraskis hologgers have access to them, and I want to collect more ammunition to spread Foster and Ezren's innocence." She tucked the rest of the cheesy morsel into her mouth, chewing with an almost challenging glint in her eye. "Which is *the truth* by the way."

Lowell sat back and crossed his arms, his forearms flexing beneath his rolled sleeves. "All right then. I also want whatever information you have on Ezren's terraforming movement—origins, goals, funding numbers, sponsors... everything."

"Okay, weirdly, I've got that stuff." Micah took another cheese stick, brow furrowing. "What about Foster?"

"What about him?"

"It might be more of an eye-catcher to focus on him. Even with Ezren's latest VSoc explosion, he's arguably more popular and one of the biggest celebrities Belethea has."

"Maybe. But Ezren's the one doing all the talking. I have a feeling if this situation was politically motivated, it has to do with her."

"But Vieve's murder occurred months before Ezren even tried out, *and*"—Micah stabbed the air with a cheese stick—"she was Foster's double."

"Oh, all right." Lowell spread his hands as if finally giving in. "If you want so badly to tell me about your celebrity crush too, you can."

Micah gasped in horror. "He's *not* my celebrity crush!"

"You have an entire hololog dedicated to him." Lowell took a stick of cheese with a smug grin, obviously enjoying getting a rise out of her.

Micah's teeth practically welded together, and she barely managed to force the words out. "It's dedicated to the Belethean team."

"So is your royaler crush on someone else then? Simon Grady maybe?"

"I don't have one," Micah snapped, half tempted to throw a cheese stick at him.

He paused as Micah's basket of spiced fries rose through the table, his brows quirked with what looked like genuine confusion. "But I thought that was the whole point of BRR hologs."

Micah narrowed her eyes, unsure if he was baiting her or if he truly didn't know. "While many royale hologs do focus on relationship aspects, mine covers all facets of the team, to include relationships, performance, and lifestyle." She shoved the fries toward him, and to her surprise, he actually took one.

"And you're going to fit politics in there too now?" Lowell asked. "Isn't that a little too serious for your brand? Too *boring*?"

"I think I can pull it off better than *some* people." Micah hooded her eyes with an imperious stare as she sipped the water from her glass. "Besides, I thought you said you were going to have an open mind in this meeting."

"I do have an open mind, but I'm still allowed to ask questions." Lowell leaned back once more, his gaze skating across the frosted panels. "Of the two of us, I think I'm the only one with any real objectivity when it comes to the BRR. I make decisions based on facts, while you, on the other hand, would pick Belethea no matter the circumstance."

"Well yeah." Back on familiar ground, Micah's shoulders relaxed. "Because I'm a fan with a soul. I have faith."

"And I'm happy for you, truly," Lowell said, taking another fry. "But however much soul or faith or whatever espresso shots you run on, I want to make it clear, I'm here to trade facts, and facts alone."

For a moment, Micah only stared at him, her water glass cold in her hand. Was this guy really that cut-and-dried? "Chaff. What're your siblings like?"

Lowell's face wrinkled in confusion as he took a swig from his own cup, Adam's apple bobbing. "Why?"

"Because I'm just confused how you, the alleged unbiased one or whatever, ended up with an opinion piece."

"Well, my sister has strong thoughts about everything, but her specialty is in the world of finance." Lowell let out a sigh, swirling the water in his cup. "My brother Roland is mostly concerned with keeping our brand on track, and my other brother Joss believes catering to the winners will let our star rise... Belethea not included."

Micah forced herself not to rise to *that* particular bait. "And you're different because..."

His steady brown gaze held hers, and her gut performed an unexpected flip. "I think truth is more important than status, fame, or money," he said.

Suns, his lofty ideals were going to make her puke. She couldn't wait to find out just how much of a hypocrite he was. "And you look down on the fan hologgers because you think we're full of chaff?"

Lowell let out a chuckle as she snatched another cheese stick. "I've seen your hololog. You're honestly selling gossip as entertainment, and you do it well. I have no problem with that."

Micah's chest warmed with the compliment—which was, of course, ridiculous. For all of his talk of truth, he was undoubtedly buttering her up to get what he wanted.

"It's the ones that sell gossip as the truth that I have a problem with," Lowell finished, his deep voice taking on an almost harsh edge.

And Micah was surprised to find for the second time that night, she completely agreed with him. "Okay." She crossed her arms. Even if he was speaking sense, she couldn't ignore how different they were. They were coming from two completely different sides of the playing field with completely different agendas—temporary allies at best. "But I still don't trust you."

He held her stare. "Well, at least we have that much in common."

Micah's lips twisted, and she forced herself to repress a smile. It was quite clear that she, a self-proclaimed rabid fan, and this alleged fact-spitter were not destined for friendship under anything resembling normal circumstances. But for some reason, she couldn't help but like him. Bizarre. Maybe she was sick or something?

She gave him a lazy shrug. "Perhaps this partnership will be fruitful after all then."

He mirrored her nonchalance, pushing the curls away from his brow. "I'm willing to give it a shot if you are."

Honestly, Micah had been in since the moment he'd messaged her. But to be fair, this was going better than she'd originally anticipated. A low bar, but still. "Okay then, now that we're working together, I'm curious, what's your true unbiased opinion of Warner Calderon?"

"I think he's corrupt."

And in that moment, Micah found herself liking him just a little more. Despite the recent events unveiled by Ezren and Foster, most hologs had taken Calderon's side on instinct... but apparently not this reporter.

"Just like most politicians of means and power," Lowell continued. "But I think if we take him down, we could inspire real change. And if what she's saying is true, your friend, Ezren, could be a real breath of fresh air."

Interesting. Micah ran a finger along the dents in the table as she considered his words. Maybe he really was an idealist. "But she's just a royaler," Micah prodded.

"And how did Calderon start out?" Lowell's face once again took on an earnest cast that seemed to hold her in place.

Under his gaze, her curiosity took hold of the conversation. "A fair point. But how did *you* start out? There are more profitable angles, and you're not even from Belethea. So what's in it for you?"

Lowell nodded, taking in a deep breath as if weighing his words. Micah forced herself to still, as if her trust didn't completely ride on this answer.

"When I was young, we lived on Jadov Station, and suns knew the place had its problems. There was so much infighting and corruption, but we *loved* the race royale." He sipped on his water again, his gaze distant. "When I was nine though, the Obronian and Dreitian teams got stuck in the wheels leg during a freak blizzard—completely took them out of the competition. Do you remember?"

Micah nodded, stretching her mind back to when she too was a little girl on a faraway station dreamily watching the

BRR. "They lost eight royalers between seven teams. It's still the greatest loss of life in a single BRR to date."

Lowell gave a solemn nod. "Yes, objectively it was horrible, but because of the turmoil, Jadov was able to come in third, and it was a *huge* deal." A smile creased his face, and Micah realized it was the first true one she'd seen so far. "It was like the whole station was walking on air. It made me feel like I could do anything, and for weeks, our station was so united in our pride, we had not one single act of violence."

His smile fell, and he turned the glass in his hands. "But since we were a dark horse win from a small station, none of the official hologs covered our bronze medal in a good light. We were cast as a team who didn't deserve it. Who hadn't earned their spot. So, a few years later, my brother started a press with the idea of covering all the teams equally. The four of us worked together on it, and to all of our shock, it started getting system-wide traction. So, when we had enough saved up, we moved to Belethea to be closer to the royale."

"And your parents?" Micah asked, trying not to think of her own mom and dad whom she hadn't heard from in over a year.

"Eh, they'll never leave station life. It's their home, and Jadov will always be their team. But me, I just like how the BRR can bring people together." His shrewd gaze lifted to hers, a smile still lingering on his lips. "What about you though? You're not from Belethea either."

"I've always liked the bonds between the racers." Micah grinned at the fresh memory of Sterling/Hart fighting through the insanity of the Walibista Channel and Grady/Guns winning a scrap against bigger numbers. "And the royalers' ability to do something that seems impossible. I love to see them coming together. And I guess watching the race makes me feel like I can do impossible things too. Like I'm also part of the team."

"Huh." Lowell's eyes crinkled, and she could've sworn there was something like affection in his warm gaze. "So I like the royale and you like the royalers."

She wrinkled her nose. "Wait, you can't seriously tell me you don't love Sterling/Hart. They're so pure they're basically unhateable."

Lowell laughed, a deep rumbling sound that she immediately wanted to hear again. "I don't know them, Micah. How could I love them?"

Bending her smile into a mock frown, she let out a long-suffering sigh. "And this is why I can't get into the official hologs. Everything seems so dry without that human element."

"And your dramatic hologging sounds needlessly exhausting," Lowell countered with a raised brow.

"Maybe." Micah twirled the end of a pigtail with her finger. "But this new mess is going to take us all down if we can't get to the bottom of it."

"Which is why we'll get this sorted out, and then we can go back to our own spheres. Facts and drama all separate and happy again."

He was right of course, and Micah should've been happy with that, but for some reason, his words only annoyed her. This was a business arrangement, and she couldn't just go forgetting that because he had nice eyes. After all, nice eyes were everywhere.

"Right." She projected her holos and flicked through them. "I'll send you everything I've collected so far, and I'll keep you up to date with what Ezren and Foster say about the trial."

"And I'll send you the council minutes," Lowell replied, looking through his own goggs holos. "Here's what I have from their last three meetings."

"Fantastic." Micah put their baskets on the center console

to descend back into the kitchen. "So was this meeting everything you hoped it would be?"

"It was enlightening," Lowell said, in an almost teasing tone. "Are you still regretting we met in person?"

Micah's lips twisted to one side, not at all ready to admit she was wrong. "And miss this ambiance?" she drawled as the frosted windows turned clear, showing them the lineup of dull-eyed, scruffy men at the bar. "Never." She linked into her tab to pay, only to find that it had already been taken care of. Well, my, my, who'd have thought an unbiased hololog could be chivalrous?

Lowell rose from the booth, his voice still light. "Maybe if you're lucky, we won't have to do it again."

"We can only hope," Micah said as she slipped out beside him. "Thanks for the snacks though."

The pub's front door slid open, and he gestured her through first, a smile lingering on his full lips. "It was my pleasure."

And as Micah walked down the street back to Carmella, she had to admit that Lowell had caught her interest in more ways than one. She'd honestly never heard of a hololog, much less a successful one, adhering to some dead code of unbiased journalism.

And even if his work wasn't necessarily her cup of tea, now she felt the need to reexamine it with fresh eyes. A bizarre turn of events for sure.

Still, she'd have to make sure to keep their little alliance from Sylvia... and anyone else. She couldn't imagine how they'd look at her if they found out she was funneling team business to *The Royaler Review* of all hologs... Even if Lowell did seem to have honorable intentions, her Belroy boys and babes would never forgive her. VSoc demanded perfection, and this was a potentially unmendable breach of brand.

But what they didn't know wouldn't hurt them. And despite everything, she was glad that she'd met Lowell Coppen in the flesh. As she ran over their conversation in her head, she couldn't help but think she'd been wrong on another count too.

Maybe he wasn't so boring after all.

Not that she was going to tell him that.

5.11.43B

Lowell: Here are the minutes.
Micah: And here's the latest from Ezren and Foster on the trial.
Lowell: Thanks.
Micah: Likewise.

5.19.43B

Lowell: Minutes again.

Micah: Holy chaff. Ambassador Villegas is driving me insane. Why does she keep siding with Calderon?

Lowell: Flora thinks it's because Belethea is fiscally connected to Calderon Industries. She can't afford for him to go down.

Micah: But he's a murderer.

Lowell: Alleged murderer.

Micah: Sigh. I still don't like you.

5.25.43B

Micah: Here's the new scoop from Sylvia on the trial proceedings.

Lowell: Wow, Ezren's and Foster's testimonies were pretty powerful.

Micah: Yeah, well, I think when someone tries to murder you, it has a powerful effect.

Lowell: Hopefully this is the nail in the coffin this case needs.

Micah: Without hard evidence? I'm not so sure.

6.01.43B

Lowell: Try not to get so riled up about the minutes this time.

Micah: I have a right to get riled up! These people are ridiculous! They're all under Calderon's thumb, and I want a new council!!

Lowell: Maybe you should make a run for it.

Micah: Would you vote for me?

Lowell: No.

Micah: You are way too honest.

6.11.43B

Micah: You're going to like this. I managed to get the BRR cam footage from Foster and Ezren.

Lowell: This is intense. With this on file, I don't know how this trial is ongoing.

Micah: That's what happens when you're the most powerful man in the system and you have a scapegoat.

Lowell: For the record, Micah, I believe Ezren and Foster.

Micah: My, my, well look at you growing over there.

Lowell: They seem like good people. I understand why you're a fan.

Micah: Ha. Not just any fan. The #1 belgirl.

Lowell: I believe that too.

6.23.43B

Lowell: Nothing in the minutes this week except admin stuff.

Micah: Shaft, it looks like they're ready to start putting the scandal behind them.

Lowell: It's probably the best-case scenario at this point. I was getting worried they'd cancel the BRR next year.

Micah: Holy chaff. Don't even say that. You're going to give me a heart attack over here.

Lowell: It was just conjecture. You do it all the time.

Micah: Yes, and in the wrong hands, you can kill someone with that kind of power. Maybe you'd better stick to your facts.

Lowell: Is this how you tell me you don't like my column?

Micah: Um, have you even been watching my VSoc channel? I love your new column. It's about me.

Lowell: No, it's about the Belethean team.

Micah: But I gave you the facts.
Lowell: Are you demanding I quote you as a source now?
Micah: No, it's more effective if I pretend I'm not involved.
Lowell: So sneaky.
Micah: One of us has to be.

6.29.43B

Micah: Just between you and me, I think I've convinced the Amaral siblings to join the Belethean team next year! SQUEEE!

Lowell: Wow, look at you pulling strings behind the scenes.

Micah: See, us fangirls have more influence than you think.

Lowell: Well, I already thought you had an incredible amount of influence, so to hear that you have more is a little terrifying.

Micah: As it should be. Mwahahaha.

7.04.43B

Micah: Wow, your columns are really catching on fire.

Lowell: Because you're promoting them.

Micah: Who knew this partnership would be so productive?

Lowell: Do I get to take credit for this?

Micah: Absolutely not. Your brother is still an asschaff. (No offense.)

Lowell: None taken.

Micah: Why didn't you write for Belethea before!?

Lowell: We're all assigned different teams.

Micah: Huh. Well make your big brother do the others so that you can write for Belethea forever.

Lowell: Ha. Thanks. I'll be sure to float that idea up to Roland.

Micah: Do they know where your information is coming from?

Lowell: Nope, I said you wanted to stay anon, so

anon you shall be... except, Flora already figured it out. She's kind of a fan.
Micah: I like her already.

7.09.43B

Lowell: How long do you think the trial will run?
Micah: At this point, my best guess is the rest of our lives.
Lowell: Are Sterling/Hart doing okay?
Micah: Yeah, they're just super busy. If you could tell your stupid relationship intern to back off though, that would be great.
Lowell: Ugh, sorry. That was Joss's idea. Flora and I are trying to get rid of her.
Micah: Can you just take over the RR already? I'd support you in a coup.
Lowell: Well that makes all the difference.
Micah: I'd be amazing in a coup!
Lowell: Trust me when I say I don't doubt it.

7.17.43B

Micah: I can't sleep.

Lowell: Then you should read the council minutes again.

Micah: I have to say, the juice I send you is much better than the proceedings you send me.

Lowell: I never said I was trading fair.

Micah: You're sneakier than I thought.

Lowell: Only for a good cause.

Micah: I'm glad we joined forces on this.

Lowell: Me too.

Micah: Go to sleep already, Viewboy.

Lowell: Goodnight, Belgirl.

7.21.43B

Lowell: I heard the storms are bad out in Tuzuno today. Are you all okay?
Micah: Of course. This is fantastic for research. We'll be on the surface all day.
Lowell: Please be careful.
Micah: Aw, your concern is so sweet, but I'm a professional.
Lowell: Then please be professionally careful.
Micah: It's okay, I'll leave a message with Ezren that she's to collaborate with you should I die.
Lowell: That's not reassuring.
Micah: I know, that's what makes it fun!

7.29.43B

Micah: Psst, Lowell.
Lowell: What?
Micah: Nothing. Just wanted to say hi.
Lowell: Hi, Micah.

MICAH'S INTO THE CHURN SERIES TIMELINE

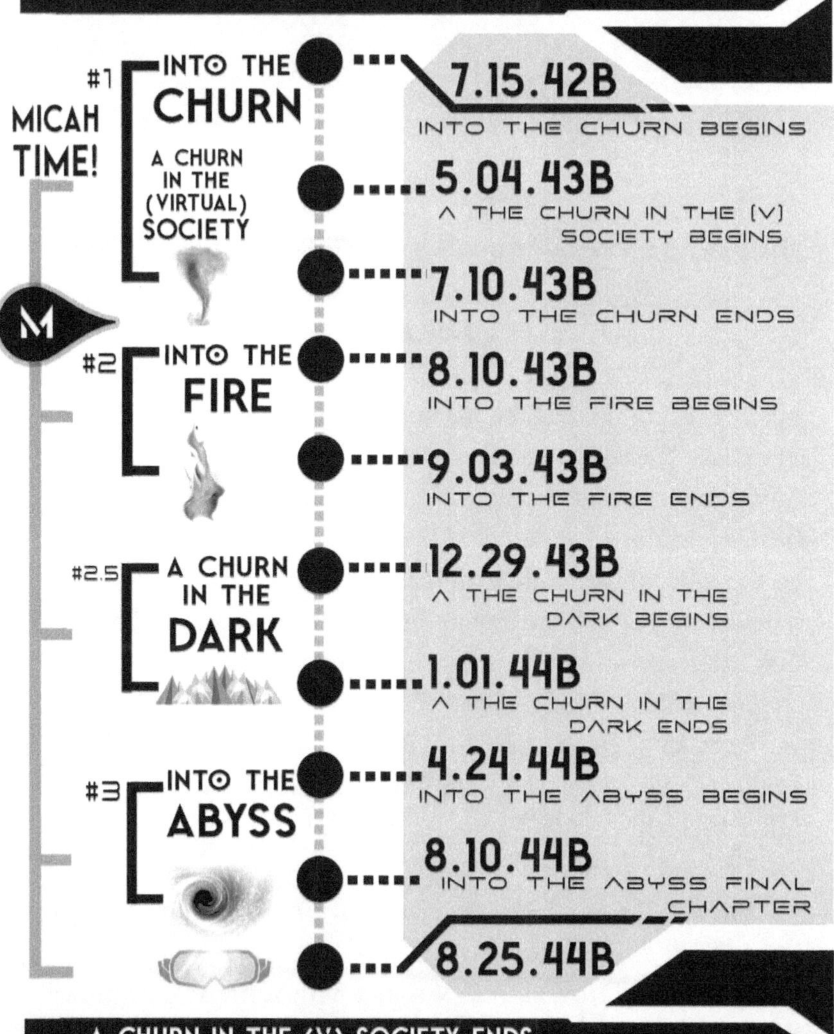

8.03.43B: T-7 DAYS UNTIL THE BRR OPENING DAY EXPO

LOWELL

FROM THE QUIET of his small, studio apartment, Lowell stared at the latest BRR Council Minutes, barely able to comprehend what he was looking at. After *The Royaler Review*'s series of Belethea, Obrone, and Calderon spotlights, he thought they'd made a difference. From the response, he'd thought they'd had an impact on public perception. Thought that after spreading the truth of Belethea's story, they could change people's minds.

FLORA: I CAN'T BELIEVE THIS. HE'S FODDING GUILTY! HOW COULD THEY LET HIM WALK!

LOWELL: I KNOW.

FLORA: THIS CAN'T BE THE END OF IT. THERE HAS TO BE AN APPEAL OR SOMETHING.

ROLAND: THEY ALREADY WENT THROUGH ALL OF THAT, FLORA. THIS IS THE FINAL VERDICT, AND THE RUMOR IS THEY'RE GOING TO ANNOUNCE IT AT THE EXPO.

Flora: We're watching the downfall of the Casolla system as we know it.

Joss: Eh, I doubt it. Seemed pretty legit to me. Lucian Talmadge confessed, and he's paying the time.

Lowell: But there are multiple eyewitnesses that say Calderon admitted to being involved, and the goggs cam for that conversation has mysteriously been corrupted.

Joss: Oh, c'mon, the people on the bottom would do anything to get a shot at the guy at the top.

Lowell: But they were all on the same team!

Roland: Enough. If this is the verdict, our series on the different takes is over. The season's about to start, so let's get back to racing.

Flora: But Joss and Lowell's back-and-forth has been really popular, Roland. They've been doing a good job with it.

Roland: They have, but I'm tired of the drama, and the constant hateful arguing in our comments. No one's listening, they're just waiting for their turn to talk, and I don't want to be that amplifier. We need to get back to what actually brings people together—the race.

Lowell's stomach sank. All that work, and they weren't expanding. After the Calderon news had already kicked him in the teeth, he honestly didn't have the energy to answer as he melted onto his bed.

Joss: Finally. I'm getting tired of the political crap. Oh, and I'm bringing the intern to the expo.

Lowell: And how does the *relationship column* bring people together?

Joss: Oh, relax, Lo. We tried your little experiment, and now we're trying mine.

Lowell: You know that doesn't fit our brand.

Roland: Drop it, Lowell. It's okay to try new things, and it's been popular. It works as a lighter distraction from all the heaviness going on right now.

Lowell's brows knitted in frustration, and with it, a sliver of boldness surged through him.

Lowell: Whatever. But I still want to cover Belethea in the racing column.

Joss: Aw, are you going soft on them?

Lowell's jaw tightened. He knew if he seemed to favor Belethea, Roland would reassign them to himself or Flora.

Lowell: No, I just figured they'd be the ones you didn't want.

Joss: You're right there.

Lowell: And you're always saying we should align ourselves with the winners.

Joss: Um, cheaters are not winners, and even if they got lucky one time, word is Sterling/Hart aren't coming back next year... so you're back to your eight-decade losing streak.

Lowell: Unless Calderon was manipulating the winners.

Joss: Chaff, Lo, stop hanging with losers, they're starting to rub off on you.

Roland: Enough. Lowell, you can only take Belethea if you remain unbiased and take on the last-place team from the BRR too.

Lowell: Done.

A private message dinged into his goggs.

Flora: Good move, Lo. It's a load of shaft that we got robbed of the political discourse, but I think the Beletheans need you.

Lowell: Thanks, Flora.

The warmth of pride flooded through his chest, but it was instantly tempered as he realized he still had to tell Micah about the latest developments. Taking a deep breath, he thought out a message to her.

Lowell: Heads up, Belgirl, you're not going to like this, and we can't publish anything about it until after the expo.

[*Attached: BRR Council Minutes 8.02.43B*]

Raking a hand through his curls, he pulled up her VSoc page in his goggs. Her heart-shaped face beamed from holo after holo—a mishmash of trial updates, Team Belethea recruitment speculation, and news of Tuzuno's revitalized terraforming efforts. Her passion and obvious love for not just the team but her fellow fans poured from the page, and he was honestly still surprised she wasn't harboring a secret crush in there somewhere.

Then again, maybe she was and just wasn't admitting it to him. Even though they'd communicated almost every day over the last three months, they weren't exactly in friends territory. Chaff, she probably wouldn't even tell him if she were dating someone. And for some reason the possibility disturbed him.

The chirp of an incoming holochat jolted him out of his thoughts. Micah was calling? Despite the hundreds of messages they'd sent over the offseason, she'd never called him. His gaze swept around his disheveled studio. A variety of mugs dotted the kitchen counter, his collection of potted plants overflowed from the balcony into the room, and his laundry lay in stacks on his fold-out bed, waiting to be put away. In a panic, he angled himself into the corner before turning on his hovercam.

Micah's face popped into the holo projected from his goggs, her Belethean-decorated dorm room filling the space behind her, and her pigtails and irises a light seafoam green today. "You've got to be chaffing me."

Lowell scratched at his head, trying to pretend like getting a call from her was completely normal. "I wish I was."

Micah groaned. "This is going to kill Ezren and Foster."

"Yeah, my sister was pretty worked up about it too."

And with a startled pang, he realized that this could be the end of their messages. After all, if the political column was over and the trial was dead, what more did they have to work on together? It shouldn't have affected him, but strangely he'd found himself enjoying her human perspective recently.

"Ugh." Micah wiped a hand across her face, and her indignation melted into slouched shoulders. "I just thought we were making more of a dent in this fight."

Lowell nodded as the questions of what they could've done differently already started to peck at him. "Unfortunately, Roland is taking us back to our more neutral stance to try to unite the people. No more side pieces."

"And he's absolutely right."

He flinched at the burning vehemence in her words. Maybe she really hadn't liked the articles after all, especially now that it turned out they'd accomplished a whole lot of nothing. "He is? I thought you'd be all about fighting the good fight."

"No, if you keep playing that game, you'll eventually be drawn down to their level. I can fight them just fine there, and even then I'm not sure there's any real winning. You need to keep the high ground with those uptight morals of yours. People listen to you because you're fair, and you report the facts. Because you don't have a slant. You need to be that voice of reason for Casolla." Her bright green gaze held his, and his pulse thudded beneath his skin. "We need that."

His cheeks burned hot in a way he hoped she couldn't see through the holo, and he forced himself to stifle the grin that wanted to stretch across his face. He knew for a fact Micah didn't say things she didn't mean, which gave her words a pleasant weight he'd be carrying around in his pockets for weeks to come. And even though he wasn't supposed to be choosing sides, he was glad she was on his.

He took a breath to refocus—there was still so much work to do here. "Okay, but there has to be some way we can be more effective. I have a feeling they're going to do something big at this expo, and when Calderon comes back, it'll be like striking a spark in the fuel tank."

Micah fiddled with her pigtails as she thought, and he tried and failed not to track the movement. "I agree, Calderon's presence will fan the flames when the bigger planets are already threatening to cancel the BRR, and we need to try to douse them. Even though you're not directly supporting Ezren and Foster, you can use the same language of unity and fairness. Of tradition. Of protecting the royalers. It's something everyone will be able to get behind, and it'll easily help us identify who the enemy is."

She smiled, and it looked almost feral. "And while you're being all honorable and sweet on the high road, I'll mercilessly cut Calderon down from below with laser precision, until only Ezren and Foster are left standing. Officially, you and I will still be at odds but with the same victim."

Lowell chuckled. "I like it." He had to give it to her; there was a reason Micah Belanger could make VSoc sing her tune. Though every holo came across blunt and forthright, underneath her manic exterior, she was planning four moves ahead. "Roland's already on that page, and we can definitely get Joss on board, but I'll have to tell Flora the whole plan to get her to budge. She's already burned up having to report Calderon's alleged innocence, but she's extremely discreet." He rubbed a hand across his smooth jaw in thought. "Do you think anyone else will notice if we're teaming up against Calderon?"

"What's there to notice? This plays right into the narrative of the standing feud between *The Royaler Review* and Belethea. We'll make sure to stagger the timing, and our messages will be naturally opposed in tone and intent. They'll have no idea." Her slender fingers drummed against her chin. "As long as they don't see us working together, we should be fine. If they do find out we're colluding, your unbiased, respectful platform goes right out the window, as does my off-the-cuff, rebellious image."

Lowell winced. He thought things would get easier from here on out, but if anything it almost seemed like the stakes had gotten higher. While unlikely, if Casolla at large *did* figure out they were working together to manipulate public opinion with a specific agenda, they'd both be done for.

"Okay, yeah, we'll have to be careful." He blew out a shaky breath. "But so far all the guesses on the anonymous source behind the Belethea column have hardly mentioned you." Which was, of course, because Micah was the one who was pretending to ferret out the traitor selling Belethea's secrets to the press. Honestly, the girl was a genius.

And she flashed a smile that said she knew it. "I guess I can add political informant to my resume."

Smothering a teasing grin, he offered a cool shrug instead. "Yeah, your latest Calderon takedown wasn't that bad."

Micah's eyes flew wide, and she leaned forward. "Holy chaff, was that a compliment of biased fangirl trash?"

"Micah." His gaze flattened. "I've seriously never called it that."

Her lips tilted up, and she pointed a green-tipped nail as if she'd caught him in the act. "But you were thinking it."

"You forget, my thoughts are completely unbiased and boring."

"What a load of shaft," Micah scoffed. "Your stuff has only gotten better lately. You get straight to the point, but you've got an edge. It just equally cuts into everyone."

Chaff, there was no way she didn't see him turning into a tomato now. He cleared his throat and grabbed his water bottle, lifting it to hide his face. "Well here's to a flourishing partnership."

Micah grabbed a bright green drink of—he didn't know what, her tone sweet and bubbly.

"May Calderon shrivel up and die."

He snorted, his face relaxing into the easy smile she always seemed to bring him. "May the truth find its way to the surface."

"Cheers."

And even though the world was threatening to burn around them, Lowell felt, between the two of them, they could do something about it.

8.10.43B: T-0 DAYS TO OPENING DAY EXPO

Lowell: Are you going to be at the expo today?
Micah: I can't make it. It's Sam Hart's first day at his new school, and I wanted to be here for him. So you'd better have good coverage since I can't be there!
Lowell: Excuse you, I always have good coverage.
Micah: Speaking of brothers, have you convinced yours to drop the relationship columnist yet?
Lowell: Still working on it, but unfortunately, she's here as well.
Micah: I'll be glad when all of this is out in the open so I can rant about that too. I'm tired of keeping secrets.
Lowell: Honestly, I'm a little jealous—the low road seems very cathartic.
Micah: And I'm a little jealous you're at the expo.
Lowell: You could always quit your day job and come work for us.

Micah: Ha. I'm holding out for the golden opportunity.

Lowell: Which is?

Micah: I'll know it when I see it.

Lowell: Okay, well, until then, I guess I'll have to cover the good stuff for both of us.

Micah: You're the worst.

MICAH'S INTO THE CHURN SERIES TIMELINE

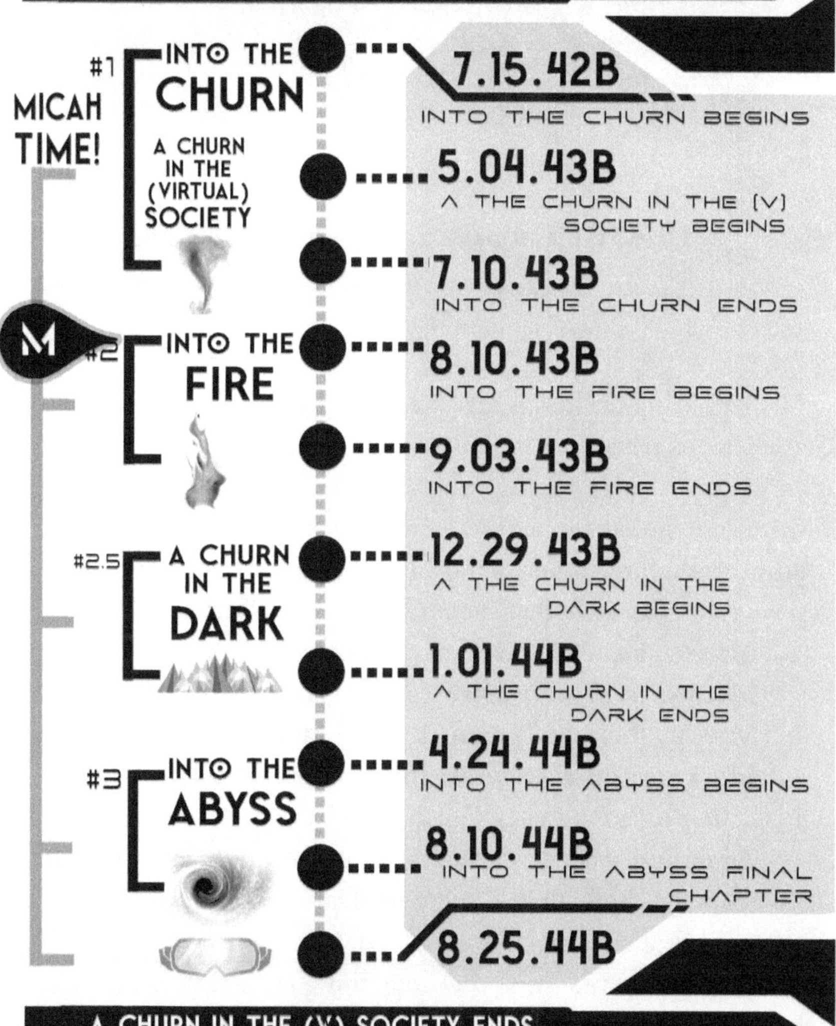

A CHURN IN THE (V) SOCIETY ENDS

8.10.43B: T-0 DAYS TO OPENING DAY EXPO

MICAH

MICAH WATCHED in horror as *The Royaler Review* and two other holos fritzed with a deafening explosion, chaos erupting as the cams spun through the air in a nauseating whirl. She froze on Belethea STEM Academy's campus, her holos erupting with messages as the fans reacted. Three heartbeats of pure panic passed before she finally leapt into action.

MICAH: EZREN!!!!!!!! ARE YOU OKAY??!?!?!!

MICAH: SYLVIA, IS ANYONE HURT?!?

MICAH: FOSTER STERLING, ANSWER IF YOU GET THIS!!!

MICAH: LOWELL, WHAT JUST HAPPENED?!?!? PLEASE TELL ME YOU'RE OKAY.

Agonizing seconds passed in which Micah berated herself for not being there. Beside her, Sam, Davis, and Dr. Evangeline chatted blithely with a group of students, because what reason would they have to think that something as benign as an expo had gone wrong? Finally, one of the holos zoomed in on Sylvia, Ezren, and Foster rushing offstage. Though scratched and bleeding, they looked mostly unharmed as the guards ushered them away. A second later, her goggs chimed with a mass message from Sylvia.

Sylvia: Thanks everyone for your concern. Though this is still a developing situation, Sterling/Hart and the rest of the Belethean team are safe.

Micah let out a minute sigh of relief, and Dr. Evangeline's concerned gaze flicked toward her. "It'll be okay," Micah mouthed. Davis laughed with the others, and a girl roughly Sam's age crouched to pet Waffle.

Heart still racing, Micah snagged Sam in one last quick hug and whispered in his ear. "I've got to go, but if you need anything, you know my comms are always open for you." She pulled back and grinned. "You'll always be my favorite fake brother."

"Like I need another sister." He wrinkled his nose playfully with their familiar exchange. "But if I did, you'd be an okay pick I guess."

"Go fritz their minds, Sammy." She reached to tousle his hair, and he dodged with a grin.

"Thanks, Micah."

With a wink and a wave, Micah sauntered off. She waited until she was out of sight before taking off in a dead sprint.

Micah: Suns, Lowell, where are you?!??

Micah: They're reporting someone died and people are in the hospital and why are you not answering?!

Micah: Lowell, answer me, shaft it! I'm fritzing out over here.

Micah: Okay, if you don't answer me in the next five seconds, I'm not going to forgive you.

Lowell: Wait, I'm okay! I'm fine! Just got caught in a little stampede there for a second.

Micah: A stampede?! What about the rest of RR?

Lowell: Everyone's fine. What about your team?

Micah: Thank the suns. They're fine too. What the chaff is happening there?

She tried to parse through the holos, but there was still nothing but chaos as people rushed to evacuate.

Lowell: They haven't released anything yet, but it looked like some kind of terrorist charged the stage and detonated a bomb.

Micah: With all those protesters, do you think Ezren and Foster were the target?

Lowell: Hard to say—Calderon was onstage too. Roland has given the thumbs-up for me and Flora to cover the whole spectrum of fallout here, so we'll see what we can dig up.

Micah swiped a hand across her face as she ran toward the storm truck station with no plan at all.

Micah: Well, this is going to be a good stage for your unity talk while I milk the Calderon-hating conspiracies.

Lowell: Yeah, the BRR council meets tomorrow so it'll be interesting to see if Obrone and Dreitis try to use this as another reason to take over the BRR.

Micah tugged on her pigtails, anxiety fluttering in her stomach as she paced back and forth in the bustling storm truck station—a high-ceilinged garage built into Honarth city's dome. The storm truck schedules spilled across the holopros lighting up the walls, but with the academy orientation going on, options to change her travel arrangements were slim. She'd have to keep her original truck to Tuzuno and settle for a late ride to Petraskis. Ugh.

The BRR was already on uncertain ground; now with this escalation, the season could be in real danger—and the Casollan political balance with it. They didn't have much holding them together as it was. Without the BRR to manage terranium rights, this could easily snowball into a war for Belethean resources. One that could tear their planet apart. Even the thought made her sick.

Micah: Okay, I'm on my way to Petraskis to interview the team tomorrow and figure out more of what's going on.

Micah paused. Should she ask him to meet up? Or would it be too weird? After all, she hadn't actually seen him since they'd met in that dive bar three months ago. Of course, it would just be a professional meeting between two colleagues. A professional meeting that no one could know about, and with so many people around for the expo, maybe it was too risk—

Lowell: Blime. Maybe we can meet up and compare notes.

The butterflies in Micah's stomach scrambled all over again, but this time in a joyous, clumsy pirouette. After all, if he was suggesting it, it would be rude to say no.

Micah: Sure, I'll let you know.

Micah lowered herself onto a sleek metal bench in the corner of the station as the chaos unfurled in her goggs. *The Royaler Review*'s feed popped back to life with Lowell interviewing some of the other attending royalers and BRR officials for their eyewitness accounts. Their rage filled her ears as they speculated on who was behind the attack, with a few calls to cancel the race. Micah pulled her knees to her chest, her blood icing over as the hovercams soared over the injured, and another Coppen sibling revealed the identity of the bomber. From a different holo, Lowell's sister, Flora, interviewed a few ambassadors on the potential effects on system tension, and the word *war* vibrated through every one of Micah's ribs.

Whoever had done this certainly hadn't had unity in mind.

She sent another message to Ezren and waited until Lowell's live stream ended before reaching out to him again. Her hands were shaking, and she was two hundred miles away. She couldn't imagine what Lowell must be feeling right now.

Micah: Are you sure you're okay?

Lowell: Yeah... I'm just... What if they cancel the BRR?

Even though he'd given voice to the fear cowering in the deepest shadows of her mind, Micah refused to entertain the possibility.

Micah: No, they *can't*. The BRR is FOREVER, terrorist attack be shafted.

Micah straightened with the words, bolstered by her own call to action as she lifted her hovercam in the air to deliver that very message to the rest of her Belroy boys and babes right there in Honarth's storm truck station.

She was prepping to go live when another message from Lowell popped into her goggs.

Lowell: With you fighting for it, Micah, I believe you.

Micah paused, covering the broad smile taking over her face. Breathing in again, she mastered her expression, thinking of the injured and terrified still in the nightmare of the expo debris. Though she wasn't certain who was behind it, she refused to let Belethea be turned from the victim to the scapegoat, and she was going to make sure everyone knew it. Her face hardened, her brows knitting together with resolve.

Only then did she blast her message to the 'verse.

After a truck mechanical failure, a storm delay, and two reroutes due to flooding, Micah didn't arrive at Carmella's gates until the early hours of the next morning, still trying to rub the sleep from her eyes. She sent Ezren another message announcing herself when an automatic away message popped in her goggs.

Ezren: Hi there, the Belethea Race Royale team is currently taking time away from VSoc for a training opportunity until the Casolla Ambassador Summit. Thanks for your understanding.

Micah frowned. Well that was fritzing weird. Ezren hadn't said anything like that when they'd talked about the explosion after she left the police station yesterday. Micah messaged Sylvia as she mentally entered the security code and walked into Carmella's lobby. Another almost identical away message bounced into Micah's goggs, and her eyes nearly bugged out of her head.

"Okay, what the suns." Brow furrowing, she sent out a group message to Foster, Bex, and Simon... only for three more away messages to fill her goggs. "No way."

She'd just been talking to Sylvia last night, and though she'd been vague about some big emotions behind the scenes, she hadn't said anything about training. They could've gone to Obrone early, but then why not say as much? Unless it was a security precaution after the terrorist attack. Micah climbed the stairs two at a time, her curiosity lending her new energy. While getting away from the chaos did seem like a good idea... why would they go without telling her? Did they think she couldn't keep a secret?

But she had one-hundred percent never leaked anything

without their explicit consent beforehand. *Or*... She gasped. Had they somehow found out she'd been collaborating with *The Royaler Review*? Coming from anyone else but Micah, that tidbit definitely could've detonated Sylvia's trust. But if someone had leaked it to Sylvia, then why wasn't it already all over VSoc? Micah peeked her head in on both the second and third floors, but only silence filled the empty halls.

Then again, maybe the away message was just for VSoc at large, and the team was still here somewhere lying low. The knot in her chest loosened at that, and as she stepped onto the fourth floor, she called out through the hall. "Okay, kin, next time can you at least let me know you're going to hide out up here before you all disappear?"

But no one answered her from the dark corridor. Her stomach sank as she walked down the hall and the automatic lights flicked on. "This better not be some prank to scare me! I'm turning on my hovercam." She drew the small sphere from her pocket and threw it into the air... because if this was a prank, VSoc would love it.

She stopped three strides from Ezren's room where the broken door hung askew. Heart hammering, she peeked into the room only to find a wreckage of graffitied hate speech, broken furniture and... suns, was that blood?!

Micah wanted to scream, but started to hyperventilate instead.

Oh shaft. Oh shaft. Oh shaft. What do I do now?

She backed against the wall, mentally flailing for the group chat.

Micah: IS ANYONE IN CARMELLA RIGHT NOW? WHERE ARE YOU ALL?

Only the five away messages answered her.

Suns, what if they'd been kidnapped?

Her chest squeezed as she gasped for air, and she sank into

a crouch. She stared at the bloodstains on the carpet, shock turning her limbs cold. She needed to call someone. Get help.

Without thinking, she started a holochat with the first person that popped into her head.

It didn't even ring once before Lowell's face glowed from her holopro.

"Hey, what's—" His brow furrowed as he focused on her, his tone sharpening. "Micah, what's wrong? Where are you?"

"I'm in Carmella," she whispered, her chest still pumping wildly. "Someone broke in but I can't reach any of them and there's bloodstains on the floor and Ezren's room has been chaffed up and I don't know what to do." With a mental command, she panned the hovercam so that he could see the damage.

"Holy shaft." Lowell shot up from his chair and started moving, the apartment behind him blurring as his hovercam swiveled to keep up. "Okay, first thing, Micah, you need to get somewhere safe. Whoever did that could come back. Get into one of the rooms and lock the door."

"O-okay." With a mental chip command, Micah opened Foster's door and slipped into his dorm.

"Good." Lowell's brown eyes softened as he left his apartment and started down an empty hall. "Now, call the police and don't come out till they reach you, okay?"

"I'm scared, Lowell," Micah whispered, her holos but a faint glow in the dark room.

"I know, but just try to hang in there." He stopped in the middle of a stairwell and looked to the cam, his gaze searching. "Listen, I'm going to hang up now, and I want you to call the police. I'll see you soon."

Micah nodded, doing exactly as instructed. The authorities arrived within ten minutes with a tidal wave of questions, but Micah had little information to give them as they combed the premises for other damage. She volleyed back a few questions of her own, but they offered even fewer answers than she had.

After realizing she wasn't a member of the team, a woman in a crisp blue uniform dismissed her with a curt wave of her hand. "She's just some hologger groupie," the woman explained to her colleague. "You know those hangers-on never know anything."

The words hit Micah like a gut punch, and she walked away on unsteady legs. Of course it shouldn't have affected her. After all, the woman was right. Micah wasn't part of the team, and she didn't have the answers that they were looking for... but the words "hologger groupie" cut her to the bone. Hadn't she worked her fingers off in the last year to try to raise creds for the team? To get them new topsuits? To make sure they had the support they deserved?

And still, apparently all it boiled down to was: just a fan.

Not part of the team.

The hateful comments from her VSoc page echoed through her all over again: gossip farmer, calamity milker, celebrity stalker... And after months of constant work, around-the-clock VSoc engagement, and endless image calculations, what had she truly accomplished? Calderon had walked free, her best friend had been the victim of not one but *two* violent attacks, and people were even talking about the possibility of a system-wide terranium war. Had Micah unknowingly enflamed the situation by stoking heated discourse?

Sucking in a deep breath, she stumbled out of Carmella's doors with wobbly steps, trying to keep herself from spiraling. Surely the team was safe somewhere. Maybe after the room got vandalized, they were lying low. But still... why hadn't Ezren told her? After all, Ezren was still her best friend, even if they didn't talk as much as they used to.

Which was fine, of course. As an athlete ambassador and

BRR champion now, Ezren was busier than ever. And so was Micah. Balancing VSoc and her day job, she'd scarcely left herself time to breathe.

Adjusting her golden pigtail buns, Micah tried to shove the thoughts away. She could comb VSoc later for clues, but right now it wasn't getting her anywhere. Instead, she pulled up the message thread with Lowell.

Micah: The police said they're taking care of it, and it looks like the reporters are already arriving. If *The Royaler Review* wants a jump on the story, you'd better hurry.

Lowell: Where are you now?

Micah: Sneaking out of Carmella's back gate.

With a chip command, the large iron gate retracted into the mauve stone walls. Mind still reeling, she stepped out onto the back alley with a strangely empty feeling and no idea what to do next. Then a shadow fell over her, and she let out a blood-curdling scream.

MICAH'S **INTO THE CHURN** SERIES

TIMELINE

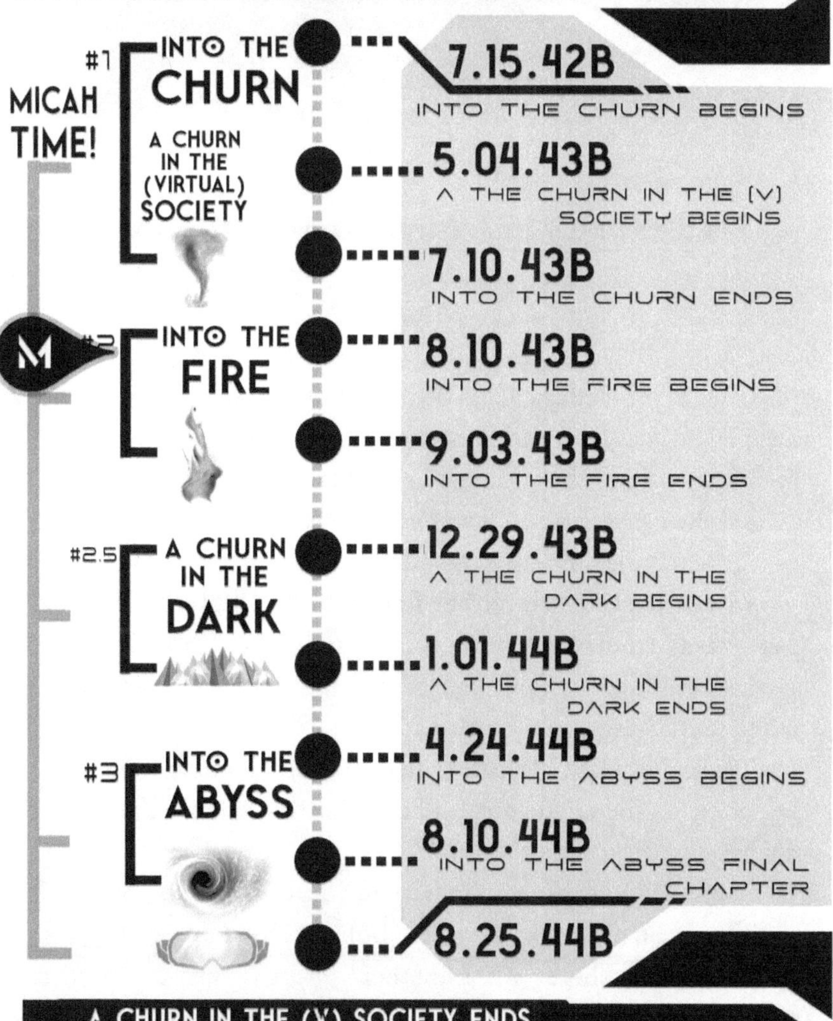

8.11.43B: T+1 DAYS AFTER OPENING DAY EXPO

MICAH

ANOTHER SHRIEK CLAWED out of Micah's throat as she jumped back against the stone wall, hands raised as if there was literally anything she could do against an attacker—an oversight in her education that she now had serious regrets about.

"Micah, relax, it's me, Lowell."

Micah peeked behind her fingers to find Lowell a full six paces away from her, his russet curls spilling out from beneath a wide-brimmed panama hat pulled low over his eyes and a white scarf drawn up over his nose.

"Asdef, Lowell." Micah folded in half, clapping a hand to her chest as she tried to calm her wheezing heart. "I'm really not great with surprises today."

"Sorry, didn't mean to scare you." Lowell's brows pinched together as he moved to her side. "But you shouldn't walk home by yourself. There was another terrorist attack at the spaceport."

"*What*?" Micah snapped straight, eyes wide. "Three attacks in two days? That can't possibly be a coincidence."

The clamor of reports throwing questions at police echoed from the adjacent street, and Lowell grabbed her arm as he guided her in the opposite direction. "It's all this discord between the Never-Terras, the bigger planets, and Belethea. It's like someone's purposely trying to tear Casolla apart." Lowell rounded the corner into another alley and paused. Pulling the scarf down, he bent to look at her closer, his gaze scrutinizing. "Micah... are you okay?"

It was only then, when Micah looked down at her hands, that she realized her whole body was shaking. Two possible murder attempts had been made on her friends in the last two days, she didn't know where anyone was, and it felt like Casolla was coming down around their ears.

"No." That one word broke down any defenses holding Micah together, and the tears burst out of her like a cracked pipe. She slapped her hands to her damp face as the overwhelming emotions rolled down her cheeks, and her breath hitched with sobs. "What if... what if they were there? And that's why they're not answering."

"No, there were no deaths reported. I'm sure they're okay."

Though this cool logic should've been reassuring, it did nothing for Micah's erratic gasps—gusting through her like a storm she couldn't quell—her cheeks heating with an embarrassment that only produced more tears. But just as she was about to flee the scene, Lowell's firm arms folded around her, cradling her against his solid chest.

"It's okay," he murmured into her ear. "Shh, Micah. They'll be okay."

Micah's sobs quieted against his soft shirt, but the torrent of worry still whirled inside of her. "But where are they? What if one of the Never-Terras took them when they vandalized Carmella?"

"No way." Lowell's voice rumbled deep in his chest against Micah's cheek. "Sterling/Hart could take on anyone. You know that."

With a sniff, Micah pulled away from him, keeping her gaze on the street. How completely mortifying. The first time she'd seen him in months, and she'd gone and cried all over him.

"Here." He handed her a white handkerchief with "LAC" embroidered in the corner, and Micah wiped her face, still unable to meet his gaze.

"I'm just worried about them," she said, voice still shaking. "If they changed their schedule, why wouldn't they tell me like they normally do?"

Lowell shrugged, stuffing his hands in his pockets as they meandered down the deserted alleyway in the quiet of the early morning. "Maybe whatever it was happened so quickly that they couldn't. Or they were advised not to for security reasons or something."

Micah's chin dipped further as she twisted the square of cloth in her hands. "I just thought I was a part of the team." But of course she wasn't. She wasn't on the roster. Not a coach or a royaler. She was just a fan. Like hundreds of thousands of others who were also in the dark right now.

"And you are part of the team, Micah. You know your hololog plays an important part in supporting their success." The words resonated with such certainty, they brooked no room for argument. "But maybe this isn't really a team thing. There's just so much we don't know."

"Right." Micah blew out a steady stream of breath, her emotions finally ebbing with their slow steps toward the main road. "But I hate feeling so helpless."

"I think we're all feeling that way a little bit." Lowell kicked at the mauve stone street, his expression thoughtful. "What about your new recruits? Are they gone too?"

Micah pulled up their VSoc in her goggs. Though technically their names hadn't been announced yet, she'd been there for every step of the recruiting campaign. "No, at least half of them are active on VSoc, and a few of them are also reporting that their Carmella move-in date has been postponed, but they're not sure why."

"See. They're part of the team too, and they're not in on whatever this is. Different team members play different roles, but that doesn't mean you're not an important piece." Lowell offered a reassuring smile, and Micah swallowed the knot in her throat, the officer's scornful dismissal still echoing in her head. "Besides the Amarals, are you getting anyone else good this year?" Lowell continued.

Micah's lips quirked up with a wrinkle of her nose, grateful for his obvious attempt to steer them to safer ground. "As if you don't know." She gave him a playful nudge, and he pretended to stagger a step.

"Okay, yeah," he admitted with a chuckle. "Best stack in this lifetime though."

She poked him in the shoulder. "You'd better be nice to them."

"I'm objective!" He pulled his scarf back over his nose as they stepped onto the main street, and Micah pulled a teal scarf from her own bag—more to obscure her tearstained face than her identity. "Not nice. Not mean."

Micah narrowed her eyes at him over her scarf, something almost comforting about their well-worn exchange. "You are nice, but *The Royaler Review* can be harsh."

"Sometimes the truth *is* harsh." His brown gaze crinkled. "I don't see you sugarcoating anything over there, drama queen."

Micah opened her mouth to retort when Lowell gestured to a large glass door wedged between a VSoc café and a goggs repair shop. "Here, I think we could use a real distraction."

"What is this place?" Micah cocked her head but didn't hesitate to step in when he opened the door for her.

The small foyer held a virtual check-in kiosk and four nondescript metal doors with various holos of trees, beaches, and mountains playing across them.

"It's a historical holo. Let's see if they have an opening." Lowell stepped up to the desk, connecting to its holopro and swiping through a few options Micah couldn't see. "You've never been to one of these?" The kiosk chimed, and one of the doors lit up green before slicing open. Lowell lifted his chin toward it with a smile. "It can recreate any place or any event from human history. Of course, it's a simulation, so a lot of it is just the AI's best guess, but we can go anywhere and anytime you want."

"Historical?" Micah raised an eyebrow as she followed him into a room showing nothing but a cloud-strafed sky above and below them. Lowell took her bag and put it into a locker in the wall with his own. "This sounds boring, Lowell."

Before she'd fully immersed herself in VSoc, Micah had enjoyed the occasional holo-theater, but those had plot and characters—a whole story you could participate in. This sounded like it could be part of a yawn-worthy history class, and while she appreciated the attempt to distract her, it would take a lot more than just some random holo to pull her mind from Ezren's destroyed room. "Besides, shouldn't we be posting on VSoc and getting ahead of the narrative?"

"You know, I hate to admit this, but I think I can safely say we both need a break." Lowell accessed the chamber's central holopro, and the sky dissolved into an underwater reef.

"Besides, you're supposed to be the open-minded one, right? So just open your mind and give it a try."

Real, actual water flooded in from the walls in a tidal wave, and Micah shrieked as she lurched toward him. "Holy chaff, are you trying to drown me? Is this revenge for hating on your boring hobbies?" She clutched at his shirt. "I don't know how to swim, Lowell."

"Just relax and put your goggs on." Lowell slid his goggs over his eyes as the water rose to waist level and two tubes lowered from a hatch in the ceiling. He handed one of the air breathers to her as he fitted the second in his mouth. Micah closed her lips and breathed the oxygen in deep as the water rose up to her chin.

Micah: I'm fritzing out, Lowell!

She clung tighter to him, and his arm circled around her waist.

Lowell: I promise, I won't let anything happen to you. Breathe and give it a minute.

The water rose over her goggs, and Micah was surprised to find... well, nothing happened. She continued to breathe, and in seconds, the small room had been completely filled with water while they still stood at the center.

Lowell: You okay?

Micah: Um, yes actually. But now what do we do?

Lowell: Look around.

Micah glanced up from his shirt to see... a whole new world. Sunlight streamed down from the surface, and a rainbow of coral surrounded them. Fish of every color darted between rocky protrusions, peeking at them curiously, and she swore she could even feel the pull of a current on her limbs.

Micah: Suns, where are we?

Lowell: Old Earth, twentieth century, Great Barrier Reef.

His eyes sparked behind his goggs as he disengaged his mag boots and floated in the water.

Lowell: C'mon, let's look around.

Micah: Lowell, I still can't swim.

Lowell: It's okay, just turn off your trainers' magnetic lock, and you'll float up. We're not actually going anywhere, but if you move your feet and hands, the room will make you think we are.

For a moment, Micah only stood there, eyeing a shark that passed all too close. She swore she could feel the movement of the water as it swam by.

Micah: I don't know if I can.

Lowell held out a hand to her.

Lowell: You can. I'm right here.

A small, orange-striped fish peeked out from a bright pink frond, and a huge turtle swam just over Lowell's head. She reached out to touch it, and—what the chaff—she could feel the slick, hard shell against her fingers.

Micah: I can feel it. How is that possible?

Lowell: The room is engaging your chip to tap into the dreaming portion of your mind and feed it the suggestions of the environment.

Okay, that was pretty crisp. While a few select animal species had been imported to Obrone and Dreitis, the holos had never seemed real to her—not like this.

Micah: And there's more?

Lowell's lips curved around his breather, his thick hair floating in the water around his head like an auburn halo.

Lowell: Oh, Micah, there's so much more.

Micah took his hand, and together they drifted up toward the sunlight. She lost track of time as they drifted between schools of fish and wandered through a pod of dolphins. They floated through forests of kelp and mazes of coral, swimming deeper until they came upon what looked to be a sunken ship.

There, Micah finally let go of Lowell's hand, swimming into the different compartments, and peeking up at him with delight. Only to flee back in his direction as an eel slithered past. A massive whale drifted overhead, and Lowell pulled her onward. A holopro flicked out from his goggs and the water retreated around them, leaving them on a sandy beach in a different century.

Taking her hand again, Lowell led her through what looked to be an ancient city. People in rough-hewn clothes went about their business as they walked through the warren of winding streets—the scents of roasting meat and rising bread wafting through the air.

They hardly spoke, except in smiles and gestures as his holopro glowed and the scene changed once again. Huge-trunked forests grew around them while deer sprang into the dappled shadow of the thick green canopy. Golden butterflies winged through the honey-scented air as Lowell spread his arms around a tree that had to be at least twenty feet wide. Micah flung herself against the trunk beside him, breathing in its fresh, fragrant scent and savoring the rough bark against her cheek. The reality of it stole her breath away.

One more change, and they ended up on the grassy slope of a high mountain, the deep lowing of cows and the chime of mellow bells haunting the air as they looked down on a town nestled in the shadow of the valley.

Her legs heavy from walking, and her clothes long dried in the warm wind, Micah sat in the soft grass. She cupped a violet flower in her palm—the delicate petals waving in the wind while insects chirruped in the gentle evening light. "Okay, Lowell, I'll admit it. This was a good idea."

Mischief tugged his lips upward. "You mean you don't think it's boring?"

"No, I really don't."

He nodded. "As a reporter, sometimes I find myself complaining about slow, ordinary days where nothing big happens." He slipped his fingers up a long blade of grass. "Sometimes I forget that the slow, ordinary days can be worth visiting too."

"Especially when they're beautiful." Micah looked out at the lush mountains rolling easily across the landscape, gentle and inviting in a way that tugged at her chest. The sight reminded her of a home she'd never known—one far away from the metal stations and intangible holos of her childhood.

And it occurred to her with sudden clarity. This was Ezren's dream for Belethea—a planet of life that they could walk freely through instead of hiding away.

"I've never been to Obrone or Dreitis, but I love going up onto Belethea's surface." Micah tilted her head, the warm sunset caressing her cheeks. "Still, I think it'd have a tough time competing with this."

"It's nice to remember where we came from, I think." Lowell turned to her with a smile. "Helps us to see where we might be going. Of what we're working towards."

Micah grinned back at him, his auburn locks falling hopelessly into his eyes and a light dusting of freckles littering his face. "Of what we're working towards." She'd almost completely lost sight of it in the day-to-day scramble, but yes—this was a dream she could believe in. One that was worth the work.

She shifted on the grass, and her hand skimmed across Lowell's. This morning she'd been ready to fall apart, and somehow he'd managed to hold her together. To whisk her from the wreckage and off to somewhere bordering on magical. Her gaze drifted over his sharp cheekbones and warm eyes—handsome and inviting in a way she hadn't noticed before—and she started leaning forward.

Whoa. No.

She turned away sharply, pulling at her pigtails as she feigned interest in a friendly milk cow sauntering their way. She could absolutely not kiss Lowell Coppen. Not here, not anywhere. Even if he was kind and smart—cute and borderline magnetic. He was a colleague—a colleague that Sylvia still thought of as the enemy, and one who had the power to ruin her hololog with a few choice truths.

Releasing a contented sigh, Lowell tipped his head back, his shirt unbuttoned at the collar and rolled at the elbows. His lips quirked in a smile as the golden glow of the fading light played across his features in the setting sun. And Micah leaned toward him all over again. Maybe not a kiss... maybe just... She rested her head on his shoulder, heart pounding and breath caught in her throat as she waited for his reaction.

And when his head leaned against hers, her ribs just about unraveled.

"Micah..." he started, his voice soft. And was that an apology in his tone? Was he about to shove her away?

But before he could say anything else, a soft chime echoed from his goggs.

THE HISTORY TRANSPORTER: THIS IS YOUR TWO-MINUTE WARNING.

"Two minutes left." Micah jumped to her feet, cheeks burning. Suns, she shouldn't have done that. In desperate need of a diversion, she pulled up the room's holo. "Oh, look, there's an option for a random selection. Want to give it a try?"

Lowell got to his feet and shoved his hands in his pockets, an unreadable expression rippling across his face that Micah didn't want to dig into. "I don't know, maybe we should—"

But Micah had already selected the random generator, and the holo melted away around them. In another blink, a cacophony attacked them from all sides—gunfire and explosions erupting in hot blasts from every direction while smoke burned her nose. Whatever city they stood in had been reduced to rubble, and bodies littered the ground, unyielding shrieks of agony and terror erupting from civilians and soldiers alike. A missile whistled through the air before crashing into a nearby building, detonating with a shower of rubble as the structure crumbled, and amidst the nightmare, a woman's cry pitched into the air.

Soldiers in bulky suits of shifting camouflage charged down the street toward them, shouting something in a language she couldn't decipher as they raised their rifles. Frustration rising, one raised his gun to strike her down with the barrel, and Micah screamed, the horror of it all hitting her in one terrifying wave.

But then Lowell's arms were around her, shielding her as he pressed her into a wall. "It's okay, Micah, it's not real." The settings flashed from his goggs, and the holo faded away again, leaving the blank sky once more.

The History Transporter: Your session has ended. We hope you enjoyed your journey through humanity's past and join us again soon in the future.

Micah gasped for breath, a cold sweat prickling her brow as she held on to Lowell for dear life. "What *was* that?"

Lowell pulled away from her, glancing at the once again peaceful sky around them, his voice soft. "It was war."

"It was *awful*!" Micah said as Lowell retrieved their things from the locker. "Why would they even have something like that in here?"

"So we don't forget." Regret canted Lowell's expression as

he handed Micah her bag. "So we don't go back." He settled his hat over his auburn hair and wound his scarf around his face once more.

Micah nodded, the scorching horror replaced by a cool resolve as they walked out into the lobby, the real world now feeling surreal after what they'd just experienced. "That's why we need the royale—to keep us from going back to that."

"That's definitely part of it. The BRR helps to focus on the things that bring us together. But it's also why we need to have news sources that shed light on the facts, even in divisive times."

And no matter what, it was something Micah wouldn't stop fighting for. Even if she was just a fan, she would do everything in her power to uncover the truth and save the race she loved. Not just for herself and her friends, but for Casolla too.

Lowell paused in the lobby, the street now busy with the lunch rush. "Speaking of, are you going to the summit next week with the team?"

"No." Micah sighed as she rubbed a hand across her brow, trying to bring herself back to the present. She checked her goggs, surprised to find they'd only spent two hours in the holo. "I'm actually headed to Lenosin Outpost in a few hours to run an experimental test series this week, and even if I wasn't, my travel budget stretches nowhere near as far as Obrone."

"Neither does ours," Lowell said. "But whenever you're in town next, maybe we can meet up to compare notes again."

"I'd like that." The words were so automatic, Micah didn't have time to second-guess them as they escaped her lips. "And perhaps we could take another break as well."

Lowell's eyes crinkled, and a smile stretched across Micah's face as she turned to leave. Even hours later when she stepped onto the storm truck, her mind was still spinning through the day and how soon she could return to Petraskis. How soon she could see Lowell again.

Lowell of *The Royaler Review*—Belethea's number one VSoc antagonist that she was definitely not supposed to be seen with.

In public at least.

And that thought had her stomach doing all kinds of flips again, leading her to an undeniable truth. She was falling for Lowell Coppen. And if anyone found out, they were going to have a *big* problem.

Just chaffing great.

8.12.43B

Lowell: Any word from Sterling/Hart & the rest?
Micah: Nope. Any word on the attack at the spaceport?
Lowell: They say it's syndicate related, but they're not connecting it to the Belethean vandalism or the expo terrorist.
Micah: Everything is stupidly suspicious but we still don't have any leads.
Lowell: Hang in there—something will turn up.

8.15.43B

Micah: I FOUND THEM.
Lowell: Holy chaff—where?
Micah: It's weird. They've already taken down the footage, but I saw Ezren, Sylvia, and Bex on Exa Station with some unidentified guy. It looked like someone was shooting at them, but they were able to get away.
Lowell: Shaft. Shooting on Exa Station? Got to be one of the dark syndicates. But why do they care about Sterling/Hart?
Micah: I have no idea. But then I found this clip too.
[Exa Station Port footage of Sterling, Banda, and Grady]
Lowell: So they're not together? That's bizarre. I wonder who that un-ID'd guy is.
Micah: I don't know, but it seemed like they were going with him willingly.
Lowell: And the stations have been scrambling

after the terranium announcement on Otho. Do you think that's connected?

Micah: I don't know how any of this is connected! And now Ezren and Foster have disappeared again!!

Lowell: I have a feeling this is bigger than we think.

Micah: That doesn't make me feel better.

Lowell: It'll be okay. They're obviously able to take care of themselves, so try not to worry.

Micah: But Otho is a nightmare planet of volcanic activity!

Lowell: I'm sure they're not actually going there.

Micah: Then obviously you don't know Ezren.

MICAH'S INTO THE CHURN SERIES
TIMELINE

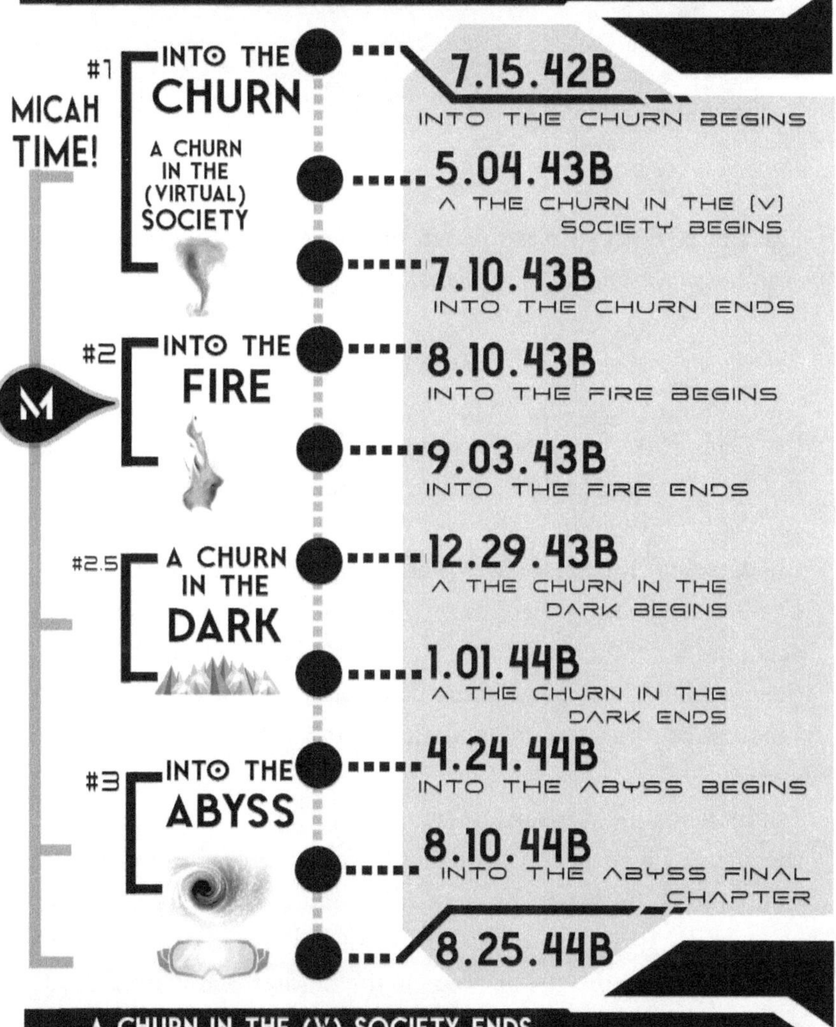

8.18.43B: T-0 DAYS UNTIL THE CASOLLA AMBASSADOR SUMMIT

LOWELL

IN THE END, the news dropped on them like a whip squall, the facts coming in like scattered shrapnel from *The Royaler Review*'s new political contacts. First, there was the news that the Casolla Interplanetary Federation was heading toward Otho and shooting terranium pirates on sight, which Lowell accepted with a tense sort of interest. He funneled the information to Micah, but her comms were intermittent from Lenosin Outpost as the brink of war ticked toward them with every minute.

However, it was only when Ezren Hart was charged with the theft of a spacecraft hurtling toward Obrone's atmosphere that Lowell shot up in his seat. His mind racing, he called and messaged Micah dozens of times but still couldn't reach her. When Sterling/Hart's address at the summit went live, all of the Coppens lost their chaff at once as they scrambled to cover the story from a million miles away—headlines bursting from their holos.

The first sentient life, luxopodos, discovered on Otho.
Baxter Industries cover-up tied to Ambassador Oliver York and the Kalashnik syndicate.
Dozens of deaths reported after Otho skirmish amid volcanic eruption.
Sterling/Hart call for luxopodos protection after the death of Ezren's father, Milo Hart.
Syndicate violence at Gobrion Station tied to illegal Otho operations.

Lowell was so caught up in his work that when a call rang through his goggs, he didn't waste a precious second to check who it was before answering.

"Lowell Coppen at *The Royaler Review*," he said, not taking his eyes off his holos. Information spilled in from across the system as he and his siblings tried to organize it, verify it, convert it into an intelligible story, and send it back out into the world.

"Lowell."

His name on Micah's lips had his head jerking up to see her pixelated shadow blurring as she ran through some kind of metal corridor. "I just got your messages. You were right. This is... it's so much bigger than I imagined. But Ezren's dad..." Her voice cracked. "My heart is just breaking for the Harts."

"I know," Lowell said. Even though, in truth, he really hadn't dug down to that human level yet. He was too caught up in the story that the system had just narrowly avoided all-out war over terranium that didn't exist. "Are you still at the outpost?"

"I am, but comms here are terrible, and I want to see if I can reach Ezren or someone on the team. I'm getting in a storm truck to Petraskis now, and I should be there by tonight." The feed glitched, garbling her voice. "I'm just totally fritzing out. Calderon Industries saved Ezren and Foster? What do I say now?"

Lowell's heart leapt at the thought that she was on her way to him, and he did a quick calculation. It would be 2000 station time before she arrived, which gave him six hours to get his work done. "We're flailing for a grip too. It all seems too wild to be real, but they have the footage right there. When you get here, do you want to meet up to go over this?"

"I was thinking the same thing." Her words held the lightness of a smile, and his pulse stuttered. "I've already posted an initial reaction, but I'm going to review the footage in depth on the way. Can you send me your address?"

Lowell resisted the urge to assess the state of his apartment. "Uh, yeah."

"Great, I'll see you soon."

With that, Micah ended the holochat, and Lowell sucked in a breath. Micah was coming. Here. To his apartment. This time, he did sweep the room and was relieved to find there was nothing objectively wrong with it. The foldable bed also doubled as a couch, and potted plants of all types fortified his patio. Other than the tiny kitchen counter on one wall and his two-person, circular table, there wasn't a lot to it. There certainly wasn't anything he could really do to fix it before she came over—his goggs chimed with another avalanche of messages from his siblings—and he had an ark-load of work to do before then.

His hovercam swiveled as he readied to dive back into his report when he caught sight of a holo of Sterling/Hart standing in the swirl of the summit, grief and blood coating their faces.

He thought of his own parents alive and well on Jadov Station, and of Micah relatively safe in a storm truck on her way to him. Sterling/Hart looked like they'd been to hell and back, and from the account, it certainly sounded like their survival had been a minor miracle.

A miracle that a lot of their critics certainly wouldn't be appreciating.

He glanced at Joss's latest message.

Joss: This sounds like a load of staged chaff if you ask me.

And Lowell was done with silence.

Lowell: Hard to argue with Grady's holos, but you gave up covering Belethea, so I think this falls way outside your lane.

Roland: C'mon, Lowell, you know this is an all-hands-on-deck situation.

Lowell: Yeah, I do, but if Joss publishes Obrone and Dreitis's conspiracies against Sterling/Hart, I will publicly denounce it.

Roland: You can't—infighting would completely destroy our credibility.

Lowell: But what's happening now is so much more important.

Joss: If you do that, Roland will fire you in a second.

Lowell: If I do that, I walk out of here as I light the match.

Flora: Okay, everybody just chill your chips. Lowell's just saying we need to reinforce our objectivity now more than ever. And he's right. The only person who has a problem with that is Joss. So either get with the program or pipe down.

Joss: You know what, I'm done with being the bad

guy here for trying to make the *Review* more lucrative. Lowell, no need to walk, kin. I'm way ahead of you.

Roland: Joss, calm down.

Joss: You know what, I am calm. I was going to wait a few weeks, but it's become clear my voice doesn't fit here anymore. I already have another offer from Obrone, and I'm taking Viola with me, since you all don't appreciate her relationship column either, even though it's been the most popular part of the *Review* these last three months.

Flora: C'mon, Joss. You're overreacting. We can sort this out.

Joss: You can sort it out to your heart's content without me. I'll be in touch.

Joss's next message to Lowell was a private one.

Joss: And since you have such a big problem with my opinions, if you breathe a word of unverified conjecture to support your Belethean shaft, as the new Obronian VSoc Manager, you can bet I will destroy you.

With that, Joss left *The Royaler Review* chat, leaving Lowell in a stunned silence. Had he just run his brother out of the family business? A mash of feelings raced through him: guilt and panic that he'd caused this rift between his siblings, dread at the obvious threat in the last message, but also, strangely, relief.

Lowell: I'm sorry, Roland. I'll talk to him.

Roland: No, don't. We all need some space to cool off, and honestly we can't afford to waste time right now. He obviously has other plans, and we'll talk to him later.

Lowell: What if we can't cover it all without him?

There were many things he didn't appreciate about Joss, but his work ethic and productivity were certainly not among them.

Flora: Roland's right, Lowell. Don't worry about that. It's not your fault, this has all been bubbling up for a while. And this story is bigger than family drama, so let's be sure to get it right.

Lowell: Okay.

With that, Lowell forced his focus on the work. To capturing the facts and reaching out for statements—from soldiers at Otho, from witnesses who saw Sterling/Hart's flight through the streets of Obrone, to victim statements on Exa Station. There were so many pieces of the story, it was like collecting breadcrumbs and trying to piece together the loaf.

And yet they were doing it. Between him, Flora, and Roland, the story was spilling out—shocking, horrifying, and inspiring all at once. Such was his focus that the six hours slipped by like a gale in a windstorm.

So when his door chimed with a visitor, he jumped out of his seat, heart pounding.

"Hey, Lowell, you in there?" Micah's voice sliced into the quiet through his apartment's comms.

"Uh, yeah, just gimme one second." Suns. How had he not set an alarm? He swept up the five half-empty mugs from his table, dropping them into the auto-wash before racing over to his bed, folding it into the wall and refolding it out as a small sofa.

He glanced over his rumpled T-shirt, thick lounge pants, and the plant-dad socks Flora had gotten him... but he really didn't have time to change without it seeming weird. So he settled for pushing his curls away from his forehead with an impatient hand before letting the door slide open.

Micah stood on the other side, but instead of her normally vibrant colors, her hair was black today, and her eyes a gray sort of hazel. Deep shadows underscored her lashes and her pigtails hung low over her shoulders, giving her an almost vulnerable air.

"Hey, come in." Lowell stepped aside as Micah brushed past him into the place. "Sorry, it's kind of small."

"Wow." Micah explored the small room with an appreciative smile, adjusting the bag hanging from her shoulder. "So no roommates, huh?"

"Nope." Lowell stooped to pick up two cushions that had fallen to the floor somewhere in the rush and threw them onto the worn couch. "Just me. Sorry, I really should've clean—"

"Oh, stop apologizing, it's twice the size of my dorm, three times as clean, and I have to share a bathroom." She flashed him a tired grin as she dropped her bags and sank into the cushions. "I'm kind of jealous."

Lowell drew one of the chairs from his table and sat in it backwards, propping his chin on the high back. "So have you heard from Sterling/Hart? I watched your initial reaction, but I've been neck-deep in work all day."

Micah nodded as she squeezed her temples. "I wasn't able to post them until I got in about thirty minutes ago, but the team is recovering on Obrone. They sent me Simon's highlights to blast over VSoc, but he sent me the rest of the footage as well, and I still have hours to go through." Her holo flicked out from the multi-lensed goggs atop her head. "I see *The Royaler Review* has been busy too."

"Yeah, we have a ton of sources sending us eyewitness accounts." The fatigue weighed on him just thinking of the work still looming ahead.

"So we both don't lack for information." Micah reached out her arms, arching her back like a cat as she stretched. "But the question is how am I supposed to spin Calderon's involvement in this? The plan was to cut him down, but he literally defended Sterling/Hart in front of the whole 'verse."

"Hmm." Lowell tapped his fingers on his knees. "Well, the whole point of this was to protect Belethea and the BRR right? To paint unity against a villain. So what do your instincts tell you?"

Micah's lips curved in a heavy smile that didn't reach her eyes. "That there are a lot of villains. And more than that, I'm worried that Dr. Hart, an actual hero, is going to get lost in all of this."

Lowell tipped the chair forward on two legs, an idea sparking in him. "Well then, why not rally them around that? Around telling Dr. Hart's story and making sure he gets the recognition he deserves."

For a moment, Micah was silent, her gaze searching the ceiling as if the answer might be found there. "You know... for an impersonal news reporter, that's a pretty touching strategy. I think Ezren will like the idea of going back to hope."

His chest warmed under her praise. While the human stories were still more Micah's arena than his, he was beginning to grasp the impact behind the different perspectives—the hope and understanding they could bring. "I don't have any information on her dad specifically, but we are getting reports coming from Baxter associates. I'll send them your way."

"Blime." Micah sat up and her holos came to life around her. "And I'll send you Simon Grady's footage. I think you'll find their interactions with York interesting."

With that, Lowell jumped back into work, only rising to get two mugs of fresh tea for them both. They talked back and forth as they volleyed information and new sources, punctuated by both stretches of comfortable silence and a few VSoc hovercam recordings. In the next two hours, with help from Roland, Flora, and Micah's footage, Lowell put together the seedy trail Baxter had left through the stations, and Micah published an emotional tribute to Dr. Hart that VSoc immediately went wild over.

The clock had just struck 0100 when Micah finally dismissed her holos. "Shaft, I never knew her dad, and the Harts never really talked about him, but I'm not going to lie, even though they seemed to accept his abandonment, I was always furious. And now to learn that he was held against his will and a good guy all along?" She pulled her knees to her chest and rested her chin on them. "I feel like such an asschaff."

From the other side of the sofa, Lowell dismissed his holos with a wave. "You're not, you're just protective of your friends."

Micah slumped against him with a groan, and involuntarily, he thought of the last time she'd laid her head on his shoulder. In the history holo, in the peaceful green grass. The things he wanted to say to her then echoed even stronger in his mind now —the desire to pull her into his arms almost overwhelming. But when he glanced down at her, the hollows of her cheeks seemed cavernous on her too-pale face, exhaustion clinging to her lips and brow.

He frowned, wondering when the last time she'd slept was. Between trying to unravel Sterling/Hart's disappearance, juggle her job as a terraforming engineer, and post BRR content to cover for Team Belethea's absence, she had to be exhausted. Suns, he was exhausted just thinking about it.

"Maybe you should rest," his said, voice soft.

"Work and life have been a lot lately." Micah didn't lift her head from his shoulder. "But we still have so much more to do."

"Well, we should at least take a break." Inwardly, he wondered at his own suggestion. Normally when he was in the thick of work, he was the last one to suggest such a thing, but there was something about Micah that made him want to take his time. To enjoy the warmth of her beside him without VSoc hovering over them both. And to take care of her in a way he sometimes forgot to even take care of himself.

"But I don't want you to slow down because of me." Micah pushed herself upright again, smoothing her dark hair, when her stomach gave a rather impressive rumble. She put her hand over it with a sheepish smile. "Okay, well, maybe a short break."

"When was the last time you ate?" Lowell rose to his feet, the emptiness in his stomach sympathizing with Micah's. He crossed to the kitchen, pulling up his current pantry stock in his goggs. "If you can hold out for a few minutes, I'll make us dinner."

Micah wandered after him, leaning on the other side of the counter as he gathered ingredients from the drawers in the walls. "Like... actual cooking? I don't even think I own a pot."

Lowell chuckled as he rolled up his sleeves and washed his hands. "Well, you're certainly not alone, but it's kind of a hobby I guess. Helps me wind down." And something about the thought of cooking for Micah sent a new, satisfying warmth through his chest.

"Is there anything I can do to help?"

"No." The smile lingered on his lips as he ran the celery and peppers through the mincer and measured out spices. "But if you want more tea, I can refill your mug." With a mental command, he turned on a gentle lilting from the speakers in his usual evening routine. A message from Flora chimed in his goggs, and he quickly muted comms.

"Wait a minute." Micah looked around the room as if searching for the source of the deep bass. "What's this?"

"Um, music?" Lowell couldn't help but smile as he started

the rice and poured oil into his steel cooking pot. "Do they not have music and food in Tuzuno?"

Micah raised a brow. "Listen, I survive on instant meals and VSoc. This is..."

"What we call 'relaxing,'" he finished for her. "Seriously, don't you ever take a night off?" He tried not to linger on the hypocrisy of his own statement.

Micah shrugged, closing her eyes as she swayed to the music. "Yeah right. Things don't get done on nights off, and I have to compete with *The Royaler Review*." She peeked at him with a smile tucked into the corner of her mouth. "But who knew *The Royaler Review* would be such a good host? Maybe I should come over more often."

Lowell fought to keep his expression neutral, as if he weren't already fantasizing about that very thing. "You're welcome whenever you're in town." Pulse thudding, he kept his eyes trained on the food as he added in the spices, vegetables, and chicken-replacement protein strips into the pot.

"Seriously?" Micah stilled, breathing in the rich aroma of the spices as the bowl superheated them in a quick spin. "What about not being seen together?"

"Well, my apartment is well out of the way." Lowell swallowed, trying to sound casual while the rice chimed its readiness, the fresh scent of jasmine infusing the room. "It's probably less risky than being in public together." Grabbing a spoon, he scooped the rice into a bowl with the vegetable mixture and slid it toward her.

"Hmm." Micah shot him another suspicious glance as she spooned the stir-fry into her mouth. "Holy chaff. How is this so good?" Her expression relaxed with satisfaction, and she chewed for only a moment before her eyes flew wide. "Mother suns. Is this how you win over girls? With the music and the cooking. Are you some kind of ladies' man?"

"*No*!" Lowell's brows leapt up his forehead, and he raised his hands as if he could fend off the accusation. "I swear, I lived with my brothers until last year."

Micah crossed her arms. "Uh-huh."

"I'm *really* not like that," Lowell spluttered, knowing his face had to be turning all fritzing shades of pink. "In fact, I think you're the first girl not related to me I've had in here."

"Really? Just me?" Skepticism oozed from Micah's down-turned mouth, but she picked up the spoon and took another bite. "But why?"

"Um, I don't know. I guess I've mostly been focused on work." Lowell served himself a bowl, trying to subtly suck in oxygen after it seemed to have all been vacuumed out of the room. "Why the third degree?" He gestured to the small table, and she perched on the chair across from him as if poised to flee.

"Because if girls knew about this"—she waved her spoon at the bowl, then vaguely in his direction in a way that did not calm his pulse—"they'd be lining up at your door."

He snorted, finally relaxing enough to take a bite. While good, he still needed to experiment more with the cayenne ratio. "I seriously doubt that."

He opened his mouth to steer them to safer territory than that outright minefield, when someone pounded on his door, and a familiar, feminine voice blared through the room. "Lowell!"

Micah clapped a hand over her mouth, her eyes sparkling with something between mischief and victory. "Holy chaff. They already know." She took another bite and lifted her eyebrows with a smug grin.

"Shaft." Lowell shot to his feet. "It's my sister; lower your voice." Connecting to the door comms, he tried to force himself to act normal. She lived down the hall so it wasn't uncommon for her to drop by, but he thought she would've been asleep by now. "Flora, this better be an emergency. It's two in the morning."

"Emergency?!" Flora practically shrieked. "We're in the middle of the biggest news drop of our lives, and you've muted your comms. I had to check and make sure you weren't dead."

"Well, I'm not dead, so you can go home now," he called.

"Why do I have to stay quiet?" Micah whispered from the table. "I thought you said your sister was in on..." Her finger toggled between them as if searching for a word. "This."

"Not good enough, it could be a hostage situation." Flora's voice blared through the comms again. "I have to see your face to verify proof of life!"

"Just... give me a minute!" Lowell sighed and rested his forehead against the cool metal of the door. "If she comes in and sees you here, she will never leave." He tossed Micah a pleading look over his shoulder. "I hate to ask this, but could you please hide?"

Micah stifled a laugh with her fist. "Um, okay. But where?"

"Out on the patio should work." He shepherded her to the glass door and slid it open with a mental command. She stepped out in his veritable forest of plants with a bemused expression on her face. "Don't worry, this won't take long."

Micah smirked. "You know, if it's an admirer, I could just leave you alone."

He gave her a flat stare before frosting the glass and turning on his heel. He'd barely made it a step before the front doorway slid open, and Flora strode through it.

"What the chaff? I didn't say you could come in."

"You said to give you a minute, and I did." She propped a hand on her hip, her shrewd stare raking over him. "Why are you being weird anyway?"

"Because I'm work—"

Flora's gaze landed on the table with two bowls of rice, and she gasped. "Holy shaft! Do you have someone *over*?"

"No." He moved to block her view of the bowls, but his sister's face lit up like a predator sighting its prey.

"Is it Micah Belanger?" She looked around the empty apartment, and Lowell moved to block her view.

"*No.*"

"Holy chaff, it is." She tried to push past him, and he pivoted to keep her at bay. "Is she here right now?"

"No, Flora!"

"I've always wanted to meet her!"

Lowell grabbed her by the arms to keep her from tearing his apartment apart from top to bottom. He looked straight into her brown eyes, like looking into a female reflection. "Flora, *no*."

Finally her shoulders fell, and she patted his arm. "Oh, fine. You're no fun. I just know you've liked her forever, and I'm excited to—"

"*Goodbye, Flora!*"

He turned her around and unceremoniously shoved her out the door—her giggles cut off as it slid closed.

Face burning and pulse sprinting, he turned to see Micah peeking through the open patio door and had to suppress the urge to slap a hand across his face. He didn't have to ask to know she'd heard everything.

And he wasn't sure he'd ever wished for the floor to swallow him more than in that moment.

MICAH'S INTO THE CHURN SERIES TIMELINE

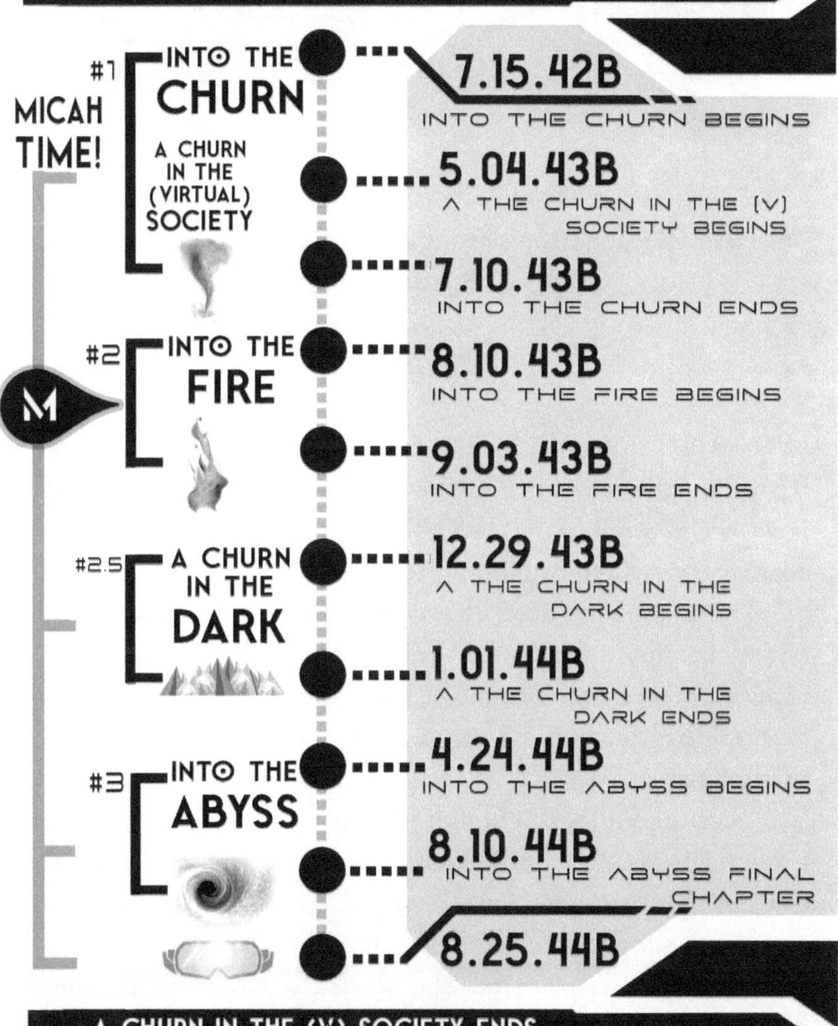

8.19.43B: T+1 DAYS SINCE THE CASOLLA AMBASSADOR SUMMIT

MICAH

MICAH STOOD FROZEN where she peeked into the room from the patio door. What had his sister said? *I know you've liked her forever?* Holy chaff. The butterflies in her stomach swirled around her thrumming heart.

The apartment door closed, and their gazes locked, his cheeks flaming a bright red. While she wouldn't have dared assume as much before, now the truth was scrawled all over his face. He had feelings for her, and suns, if it wasn't the cutest thing she'd ever seen.

"Sorry about that." He propped his hands on his hips with a deep sigh, his attention suddenly darting back to the bowls on the table. "My sister is... embarrassing."

Micah slipped into the room, tipsy on a heady mixture of exhaustion and excitement. She needed to tread lightly here, but that was toooootally not her strong suit. "So..." She closed the patio door behind her with a soft click and rocked back on her heels. "How long have you had a crush?" Okay, not exactly subtle, but there wasn't a 'verse where she could be subtle about this.

Shoving his hands in his pockets, he leaned against the closed door as if accepting defeat. "I don't know. Sometime between when you walked in and out of Dak's Pub."

Micah closed the distance between them slowly, carefully. Keeping her expression neutral even as her heart leapt at his admission. "But that was months ago."

"Look." Lowell pushed his mass of auburn curls out of his eyes. "I know it's awkward, and I promise I won't act on it, so can we just pretend that none of this happened?"

But Micah only grinned as she took another step forward, and if she looked half-manic now she couldn't help it. Excitement wasn't an emotion she was in the habit of suppressing.

The beat of silence stretched between them before Lowell's brows knitted in suspicion. "What?" Micah's grin only widened, and his lips tugged up in kind. "Seriously, what?"

Only a step away now, Micah gave him an innocent shrug. "I don't want to pretend it didn't happen." She didn't do well with uncertainty, but now that she knew his side of it, there was clearly only one course of action.

His face fell. "Oh, well I underst—"

"Because I've been crushing on you too." Micah drank in the shock in his eyes, her words obviously not processing as she closed the distance between them. Bracing her hands on his chest, she lifted up on her toes and planted the brush of a kiss on his lips in a silent question.

For one long heartbeat, they remained frozen there, balanced on the fulcrum of a moment.

"Micah." Then, as if her whispered name was the key, he came unbound.

His hands rose to cradle her face while his warm mouth

moved against hers in earnest. She pressed closer, her hands tunneling through the thick, russet hair she'd been longing to touch since she first saw it falling into his eyes. She tugged softly on his lower lip with her teeth, and a low groan rumbled from his chest. He slid his hands around her waist and they turned until his body pressed her against the door, the heat between them growing into a feverish pitch.

But just when Micah thought she'd completely lost control, he pulled back ever so slowly—his eyes hooded with reluctance. Micah had to stop herself from clutching him back to her because suns, who thought there could be a kiss as blime as all that?

"I don't want to make things more complicated for you," he whispered, his fingers tracing the exposed skin beneath the tail of her shirt in a maddeningly seductive motion.

Still breathless, Micah grinned, her hands playing over the muscles in his back. "Complications make us feel alive." And after that kiss and the scorching heat of his touch, there was no way she was going to walk away from this. She didn't even know if she could. While she'd had dallying relationships and dozens of cursory interests, none of them compared to the fire sizzling between her and Lowell at that moment.

He smiled, placing a lingering kiss on her jaw, his voice soft. "I'm certainly feeling alive right now."

His words bolstered her with an intoxicating sort of courage, her mind racing ahead to possibilities. After all, they'd already wasted months they could've spent together, and she was determined not to lose another day.

"It's a good feeling, isn't it? I think I could get used to this." She leaned back against the door, holding his gaze beneath her long lashes. "You being *my* complication."

He traced the curve of her cheekbone down the slope of her neck. "As long as I'm yours."

Their lips met again, slow and sumptuous—as if they'd suddenly decided they had time to savor the moment. To taste it, drink it in, explore this uncharted territory with warm lips and light fingers. And Micah had the ridiculous thought that maybe they could live in these long, breathless minutes forever.

But then her goggs chimed.

Micah groaned as Lowell pulled away, and she checked her goggs. "It's Sylvia." She was about to dismiss it when she caught the words on the screen. "Oh suns, it's a list of politicians they think might be implicated with Oliver York."

"It's okay, we can get back to work." Lowell's lips canted in a bittersweet tilt, and he pressed a kiss to her brow. "We'll have more time later, and Flora would probably charge over here and kill us both if I held out on her."

Micah nodded, and while there was a part of her loath to move past the inferno that had lit between them, she couldn't ignore why she was here. Couldn't ignore the blaze that was burning through the rest of the 'verse in an entirely different way. Besides, Lowell was right, there would be plenty of time to explore the fire between them after they finished their work. With that thought in mind, she and Lowell managed to transition almost exactly to where they'd left off.

They finished dinner and leapt back into the avalanche of information. But this time soft touches and shy, sweet glances punctuated their conversations. It was well past 0400 when Micah's eyes began to droop closed despite her best efforts, her chin dipping toward the floor where she lay sprawled on her stomach on the rug—holos glowing all around her.

"You should get some sleep," Lowell whispered from where he sat against the wall beside her.

"I have to keep working." Yawning, Micah let her cheek rest on the crook of her elbow. "There are still so many messages and footage and data to go through." Her words slurred with exhaustion even as she tried to focus on the names in front of her. When Lowell spoke again, his voice seemed to come from far away.

"Okay, why don't you just rest for a few minutes, and then you can get back at it."

Micah didn't open her eyes, the insistent tug of sleep pulling her under on the thick rug. "Just for... few... minutes."

She just barely surfaced from her doze to register Lowell scooping her up and moving her to a bed. She automatically snuggled deeper into the blankets, gratitude and relief overpowering any other thought. Through the haze of sleep she wasn't sure if it was her imagination as Lowell pressed his cool lips to her brow, voice soft.

"Don't worry, I've got the rest."

And with those sweet, reassuring words, Micah drifted off into a dreamless sleep.

Micah woke to Petraskis's simulated sunlight beaming through the glass patio door, bathing the verdant potted plants in gold. She blinked blearily while she tried to get her bearings —tracing her steps from the outpost, to the storm truck, to her and Lowell's near all-nighter.

Lowell.

She touched her lips as their heated kiss replayed in her head, but where was... Micah's lips curved in an affectionate smile when she caught sight of Lowell slumped over on the table. Dozens of mugs surrounded him, and his holopro still glowed from his goggs. How much later had he stayed up working?

It was only then that panic sang through her as she thought

of all the information she'd left undone with Sylvia, Ezren, and Foster counting on her to get the story straight. She tapped into her overflowing messages... only to find dozens of comms from both Lowell and Flora. Suggestions on posts. Information she could use. The leads that had panned out and those that hadn't. Other hologgers she could contact to spread the story.

She sat up in shock, the thick blanket falling away from her shoulders. They *had* done everything, and the last message was from only twenty minutes ago. Another notification chimed in her goggs with the reminder that her storm truck left for Tuzuno in an hour. *Shaft.* She couldn't miss it, not when messages from Sam and Dr. Evangeline were also filling her goggs.

With a regretful sigh, she moved to the table and rested a hand on Lowell's back. His eyes flew wide, and he bolted upright so suddenly, Micah let out a shriek.

"I'm awake!" he said. "I swear I'm awake!"

"Suns, Lowell, you scared me!" She swatted him playfully on the shoulder. "And you shouldn't be awake at all; you should be asleep."

His shoulders relaxed when he saw her, and his head started to droop toward the table once more. "I mean, if you insist."

"No, no, no." Micah tugged on his arm and pointed him toward his bed. "You sleep there."

Rising, he regarded her with a half-lidded gaze. "But where will you sleep?"

She wrinkled her nose, regret tinging her words. "I have to go; my storm truck leaves for Tuzuno in an hour."

"Ah." He straightened, a small glint of clarity coming back to his eyes.

She tugged on the collar of his shirt. "But I hope I don't have to wait for the next crisis to see you."

He softened once more. "Come here." Micah let him gather her in his arms, his stubble-roughened cheek brushing against her smooth one. "Thanks for coming, Belgirl."

"And thank you, Viewboy... for everything." She wound one of his soft locks around a finger. "When do you think I can see you next?"

"I could come to Tuzuno to do a piece on the royaling conditions there."

"And I could come back to Petraskis to meet with the university here on their terraforming research." Micah grinned up at him. "But only if you cook for me again."

He pressed a soft, slow kiss to her forehead and then another to her cheek. "Every time."

Micah's goggs chimed again, and reluctantly she opened the door behind her before stepping into the hall. "Let me know when you drop into Tuzuno."

He caught her hand, drawing her back for one last lingering kiss that threatened to melt her bones. "As soon as I can."

"Still not soon enough." She smirked back at him as she backed away before all willpower left her. "Now get some sleep before I tell everyone *The Royaler Review* is run by a bunch of workaholics."

He chuckled. "Bye, Micah."

Micah couldn't help looking over her shoulder as she walked away, his gaze following her until she disappeared around the corner. Leaving his warm, welcoming arms was so hard when the world was unbelievably snarled around them. But this thing she had with Lowell was the best she could remember feeling in a long time, even if their kisses felt stolen in the midst of a storm of work.

He made her feel like they were doing something worthwhile. That she could do anything. In a 'verse of billions—of politicians, and celebrity royalers and millionaires—his gaze trailed after her like she, a Belethea fangirl from the Pyrrhia Station, was the center of it. She flicked through the coverage he'd posted of the summit, each piece fair and factual, and she swelled with pride.

Because in a world with so much darkness in it, Lowell Coppen was a steady light.

And with him illuminating the shadows, maybe they could all find the strength to keep untangling the mess after all.

9.01.43B

Lowell: I'm coming out to Tuzuno tomorrow. Can I see you?

Micah: Already looking forward to it. I get off at 1700 station time. Meet you at my dorm room?

Lowell: Are you cooking this time?

Micah: Not on your life.

Lowell: Then I'll pick up dinner on the way.

Micah: Be careful. If you keep talking like that, I might just keep you.

Lowell: I'll keep it under advisement.

10.17.43B

Micah: I'll be in Petraskis in two hours.
Lowell: And I'll be meeting you at the station.
Micah: You can't! Someone will see you!
Lowell: Aw, c'mon, no one will notice. I've got a hat and scarf to hide my face.
Micah: Well, okay, as long as you're careful.
Lowell: Now, that didn't take much convincing.
Micah: How about that.

11.08.43B

Lowell: So when do you get back this time?

Micah: I've got another three weeks in the middle of nowhere. I'm getting good data, but I miss your face.

Lowell: You miss me?

Micah: Um. Yes. Of course I miss you.

Lowell: And you want to see me?

Micah: Pretty sure I would cut off one of my pigtails right now to see you.

Lowell: Okay, well don't cut off your pigtails... but maybe you should come open your door.

Micah: WHAT?!! YOU'D BETTER NOT BE JOKING RIGHT NOW.

12.03.43B

Micah: I JUST GOT INVITED TO GERARD & GRETA'S NEW YEAR'S EVE PARTY!
Lowell: I am both excited for you and incredibly jealous at the same time.
Micah: Sorry I won't be able to meet up for New Year's though. :(
Lowell: But you'll be in Petraskis... so maybe you can hang out the day after?
Micah: ...What about a few days after?
Lowell: It's a deal and no take-backs.

12.30.43B

Micah: Are you seeing what's happening to the Amarals?
Lowell: Yes, Roland's on site, but he says the Crionian Race Royale Council is being cagey. Do you know what's going on?
Micah: Not yet, but Sylvia seems to think something's wrong. I'm crowd-sourcing ideas.
Lowell: I'll let you know if we hear anything.

12.30.43B
(ELEVEN HOURS LATER)

Lowell: So the official statement from the Crion Race Royale Council is that there was outside interference. But Roland says the CIF sent reinforcements, and there was a body?!!

Micah: Sylvia said it was Oliver York, and the Crow's syndicate was responsible... whoever that is.

Lowell: I just talked to Flora. He's bad news. Do we know why he was involved?

Micah: Sounds like he's trying to manipulate Ezren and Foster.

Micah: Holy chaff.

Lowell: What?!

Micah: Sylvia just officially offered me a job as the lead Belethea VSoc Manager.

Lowell: Congrats!!!!!! That's completely blime!! You accepted, right?

Micah: I did... but what does that mean for us? I mean, dating a fan hologger is one thing, but dating the official hologger for the Belethea team? There has to be some kind of conflict of interest there. If your brother caught wind of it, he'd kick you out of *The Royaler Review*, and I can't even imagine how betrayed Sylvia would feel if she found out.

Lowell: It'll be fine, Micah, we've been doing this for months now. We'll manage it, I promise. For the moment, let yourself be happy. This is that golden opportunity you wanted, right?

Micah: It's the opportunity I didn't even let myself believe was a possibility.

Lowell: Then be happy, Belgirl. I'm happy for you. Always.

Micah: And you know, this means no more remote work trips, and I'll be officially moving to Petraskis. I hope you're ready to see me more often.

Lowell: I take it back, you don't need to be happy, because I'm chaffing thrilled enough for both of us.

Micah: Me too, Viewboy, me too.

MICAH'S **INTO THE CHURN** SERIES

TIMELINE

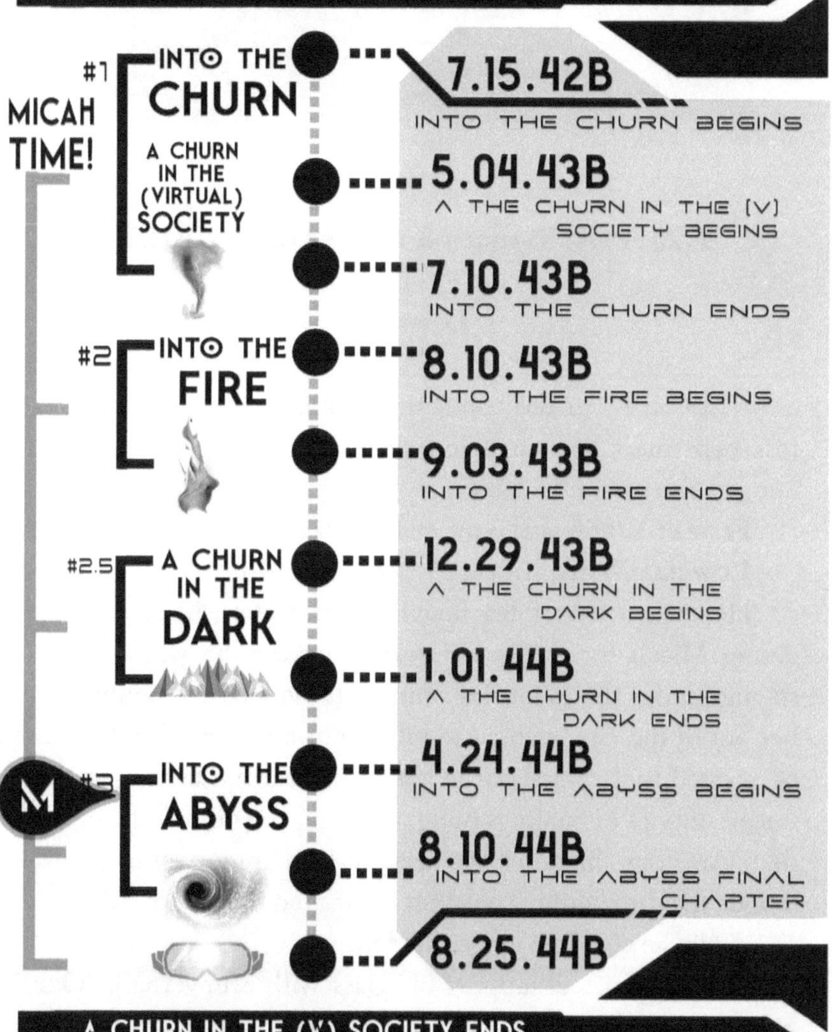

A CHURN IN THE (V) SOCIETY ENDS

4.25.44B: T-MINUS 8 DAYS UNTIL THE BRR

LOWELL

LOWELL SAT in the booth beside Flora while Roland and Joss both munched on onion rings across from them. Flora nudged him under the table.

FLORA: WELL, ARE YOU GOING TO ASK?

LOWELL: YEAH, JUST GIVE ME A SECOND.

He took a sip of his lime-flavored water. After secretly dating Micah for the better part of a year, he was tired of staying under the radar. He wanted to be able to openly take her out in the city, wanted to talk about her to his family, and he wanted to dream about moving forward. But as long as the uncertainty of his siblings hung over him, he couldn't do any of that. And the shame of the secrecy kept three words on his tongue that he should've told her a hundred times by now.

A fact he could no longer hold in.

"So," he started, tapping his glass with a fingernail. "Our political and financial articles have been getting a lot of traction."

Roland nodded as four bowls of ramen rose through the center of the table. "I think we're pretty well established now as a neutral entity in the expanded sphere, even with Joss's heckling from Team Obrone."

Joss grabbed a bowl with a superior grin. "You all can be neutral all you want while I roll in the creds for half the work." He slurped up a waterfall of noodles. "Now I don't have to write anything that isn't about the royale, and I don't have to waste my time with the teams no one cares about."

"Seems like a lot of people care about Belethea now though," Flora said with overly sweet innocence as she tied her thick copper hair into a long ponytail. "Lots of people think they'll win this year."

"In any case." Roland gave them both a stern glare. "We can now afford to hire on a couple more hologgers for more team coverage. We'll be looking for those without a large VSoc presence yet or ones with neutral stances to further strengthen our brand."

Lowell chewed through a mouthful of chicken-flavored protein, swallowing before he spoke. "Yeah, but now that we're better established, I think we have more flexibility."

"Right," Flora continued. "Like if one of the new hologgers had a personal connection to a team, it wouldn't be a big deal."

"A personal connection?" Joss snorted. "You mean like they have a sibling on the team or something? There's no way they could be seen as unbiased."

"And why not?" Lowell's stomach sank even as he argued. "I think that would completely depend on the person."

"Why? Do you have someone in mind?" Roland asked.

"I do," Flora said, wincing as Lowell kicked her under the table. While he'd told Micah he was planning on broaching the subject, he'd certainly not planned on coming clean.

Especially with Joss here to stir the pot. Flora shot him a scowl.

Flora: I'm trying to help you.

"But the, uh, candidate is dating one of the team VSoc managers," she said aloud.

Roland's brows lifted as he turned to Joss. "We're not talking about your girlfriend, are we?"

Joss chuckled, a brown curl falling artfully onto his forehead. "You'd have to be more specific about which one you're referring to, but I don't think any of mine fit your brand."

"Yeah, I think it's probably a hard no anyway." Roland ran a hand through his beard. "The BRR hologger community is relatively small, and it would be impossible to be objective if your significant other had an agenda."

And there it was. If his relationship with Micah was uncovered, he would be out of *The Royaler Review*, just like Joss. Flora shot him a sympathetic frown before turning back to Roland, her voice uncharacteristically soft.

"I think you'd look at it differently if you knew the person."

Joss glanced back and forth between Flora and Lowell, his expression sharpening. "Well why don't you just go ahead and spit out who it is. You obviously both know. Is this like Lowell's girlfriend or something?"

Lowell nearly spewed liquid all over the table, erupting in a fit of coughing.

"Wait, Lowell's dating someone?" Roland's voice pitched with incredulity. "Since when?" He turned to Joss. "You've been on Obrone for six months. How did you know?"

Joss's grin took on a victorious gleam. "Oh, c'mon. It's obvious. He never used to leave Petraskis, and now he has that weird away message all the time, but he never actually says where he's going."

Roland turned to Flora with something like betrayal grooving his face. "And you knew about this?"

Flora took a prim sip of golden broth. "I have nothing else to share at this time."

Lowell took a deep breath, trying to figure out how this had gone so wrong. "Look, we've been trying to stay out of the public eye, but no, she's not the one looking for a job."

"But... is she Belethean? How long have you been dating?" Roland leaned across the table, his wild brown hair framing his earnest expression. "We obviously want to meet her."

"Yes, do tell," Joss added, still grinning. "Somehow I have a feeling her name is going to be familiar."

Flora turned toward Lowell with an expectant tilt of her chin.

Flora: You need to tell them.

Lowell: He just said he's not going to stand for it.

Flora: You're our brother. It's different. Besides, if you don't say something now, Joss won't stop digging till he finds her, and you want it to come from you.

"Fine." Lowell set down his spoon and let out a long sigh. "Her name is Micah Belanger, she's the Belethea VSoc manager, and we've been together since the season kickoff."

Joss's jaw went slack, and Roland's spoon actually clattered to the table. At any other time, it might've been amusing, but in that particular moment Lowell's stomach only tightened.

"No fodding way." Joss threw his head back in a shocked guffaw. "The *Belethea hype girl*?!" Hysterical laughter wracked his body, his breath coming in wheezes as he turned to Roland. "If this gets out, you're totally fodded. No wonder you all have gone soft on them. It's because Lowell is—"

"Shut up, Joss," Flora snapped. "Lowell has been nothing

but impartial. We had all just agreed what a great job he's been doing not five minutes ago."

"We never said there were rules on who we could or could not associate with," Lowell said, his voice deadly calm even as rage spooled through him. If he didn't get out of here soon he was going to slug Joss right in his punchable face.

"But you kept it a secret because you knew what would happen if people found out." Roland finally met his gaze, the warmth drained from his countenance, leaving only stone behind. "And how do you know she's not just getting close to you to try to get good press for her team?"

"Don't even say that." Lowell's hand fisted, every muscle tight.

"Oh, c'mon, you know everyone will say that when this gets out," Joss said, glee lilting his words. "Chaff, *I'll* be saying it."

Lowell shot from his seat, towering over his brother. "You will *not*."

Joss lazily rose, closing the distance between them until they were practically nose to nose. "And who's going to stop me?"

"Sit down." Shooting up, Roland grabbed each of them by the collar and shoved them back into their seats. "Both of you." He sat down and steepled his fingers as he took a deep breath. "Joss, if you're the first to print something about this, I'll make sure everyone knows Dreitis is paying you to not mention them negatively."

Joss purpled. "But that's not illegal."

"Neither is dating a Belethean hologger," Lowell snapped.

"It's not illegal, but it doesn't look good, and I imagine it could be grounds for Obrone to dismiss you," Roland said.

Flora made an "oooh" noise that was decidedly *not* helpful.

"And Lowell." Roland's hard gaze skated to him. "You are

allowed to date whoever you want." Shock and relief washed over Lowell in a wave, but the heaviness in Roland's stare pinned him to the spot. "However, you cannot go public with this. Not ever. And if it comes out, you will have to immediately resign." A small gasp escaped Flora beside him. "In fact, go ahead and make sure the holo's ready to go in case it leaks. Maintain that you were impartial and that you purposely kept *The Royaler Review* in the dark."

"But Roland." Flora's brow furrowed. "You'd basically be publicly disowning him. He might not even get a job anywhere else."

"Yeah, but if Roland doesn't, Lowell would be taking down *The Royaler Review* with him." Joss took a swig from his cup, the anger in him fading as quickly as it'd come. "VSoc is a hard industry that rises and falls with the brand. If you don't fit the one you've got, you find a new one." He gestured to himself as a prime example. "Lowell's lucky Roland's even keeping him for now. It's a risk."

"It would be less of a risk if we didn't have to blackmail you to keep you from exposing him." Flora white-knuckled her spoon, looking ready to fling it across the table at any moment.

A flurry of expressions scrolled across Joss's face too quickly to catch. "I wasn't actually going to do it, Flora. Chaff. I was just getting a rise out of him. Chill your chip."

"If you dismiss Lowell, I'm going to resign as well," Flora said, her expression as grave as cold space. "Because I stand by the belief that we can keep our professional and personal lives separate, no matter what stones VSoc will throw at it."

Roland nodded with a resigned sort of acceptance. "With all three of you gone, it won't even feel like *The Royaler Review* anymore. Even if I bring on more people... the brand won't be the same. In a way, it'll be the end."

For a moment, all four of them fell silent as they stared at their bowls, and Lowell couldn't help but feel like they were falling apart.

Like *he* was causing them to fall apart.

This one confession unraveling his brother's hard-won brand, and with it, the family it had bound together

But what was the other choice? To break up with Micah? Perhaps there was a time when work would've always come first, but now he couldn't fathom putting something as ridiculous as other people's opinions before their relationship, and he refused to offer it as a possibility. Even for his siblings.

And so instead, they ate their ramen in silence, the end of *The Royaler Review* looming over them all.

MICAH'S INTO THE CHURN SERIES

TIMELINE

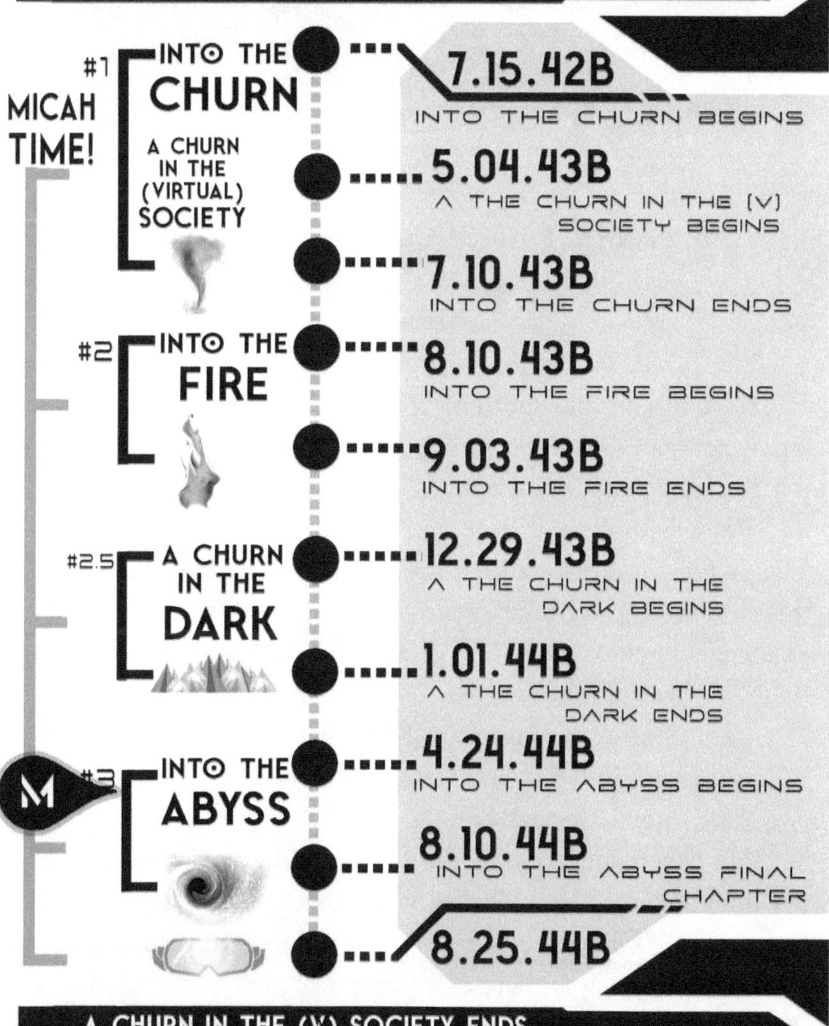

A CHURN IN THE (V) SOCIETY ENDS

5.01.44B T-minus 4 days until the BRR

Micah

IT WAS three in the morning before Micah burst into Lowell's apartment, an exhausted smile stretched across her face. "Holy chaff, I have so much to tell you!"

From behind a wall of holopros, he regarded her with a sleepy grin from where he nursed a mug of tea at the counter, his chest bare and his pajama pants slung low over his hips. "Is it about Calderon's death? We've been working that story all day."

"That's only the beginning." She bounded up to him and threw herself into his arms, the high of Ezren and Foster's wedding singing through her.

He caught her around the waist, pulling her close as the soothing notes of an old-world violin reverberated through the apartment. "Oh yeah? It must've been a pretty blime party then. But with a bunch of royaler legends at a rock star's mansion, I guess I'm not surprised." He arched a brow. "None of those Naris royalers tried to steal you away, did they?"

"Ha, they all know I'm way out of their league." Cupping his face in her hands, she drew him down for a kiss. Since she couldn't publicly admit they were dating, she did get a lot of flirtatious VSoc attention, and though Lowell had never expressed anything other than a playful jealousy, she tried to reassure him whenever she could.

She pulled away, her eyes lidded with mischief. "You can't print this yet, but Calderon's death has been labeled suspicious, and he's willing everything to Foster." While Foster and Ezren hadn't officially announced it yet, she'd been fortunate enough to overhear them whispering about it to each other after the ceremony.

Lowell's brown eyes flew wide. "What?!"

"Yes!" Micah bounced with excitement, grateful she at least had someone she could confide these juicy secrets to. "And now Foster and Ezren are married."

"No fodding way," Lowell breathed. "Since when?"

"Um..." Micah pretended to check the time on her goggs. "About three hours ago."

"Holy chaff." Lowell scrubbed a hand across his jaw, the calculations almost visible on his face. "When do you think they're going to announce it?"

"I'm not sure yet, but I'd bet that it'll come out soon. Maybe even before the pre-BRR press conference. You're covering it, right?"

"Yeah, we'll be there. I'll try to drum up a rough draft of a statement so we can get an edge on coverage. Holy chaff, Flora and Roland are going to love this."

"What do you think the Casollan reaction will be?" Micah asked, twirling a loose lock of her teal hair. While the BRR and terraforming ramifications were easy enough to grasp, the political and financial cogs of the 'verse were still mostly beyond her.

"Honestly, I'm betting pretty positive. Foster and Ezren are popular, and they've been working with Calderon for almost a year. After the initial shock wears off, it makes sense, and I think the news will settle in fine." He picked up his mug and took another sip of his tea, expression thoughtful. "With all of the policies they've been enacting, Casolla's positive trend should continue." He gave her a tired grin. "They have a chance to make the world better, and people will realize that."

After the frantic chaos of the last twelve hours, Lowell's composed acceptance soothed Micah's frayed nerves. She circled her arms around his waist once more, the warmth of him radiating through her. "I think you're the most calming person in the 'verse. No wonder people like your hololog."

But where she was expecting a smile, a shadow crossed his face instead. "I have something to tell you too. I told my family we were dating."

Micah froze. "And what'd they say?"

"Roland said it was fine as long as we keep it a secret."

"Oh thank the suns." Micah let out a relieved sigh. "I'm still trying to work up the nerve to tell Sylvia, but I think she's finally starting to come around to the RR. At least we don't have to worry about your brothers finding out anymore." She cocked her head. "But why do you not look happy about it?"

He gave her a sad smile. "Because I'm tired of hiding and sneaking around, Micah. I want to be able to tell people we're together. I want to be able to meet you at work or down the street for coffee. Not stay holed up in here."

Micah softened, her love for him threatening to spill out. The big L-word bounced around her mind, begging to be set free, but she tugged it back. In truth, she'd never said it to a boyfriend before, and she wanted to make sure she saved it for the perfect moment. Lowell deserved that, and they would have time later, after all this blew over.

"I know, Lo, and we will do all those things one day. We're figuring it out just a little at a time. But right now, your job is too important to put aside."

He framed her cheeks with his hands. "Not as important as you, Belgirl." With that, he leaned down and kissed her, slow and deep—with a familiarity that made her head spin and felt like coming home all at the same time. It was only under the touch of his lips that she completely melted against him, surrendering to the perfection that was the two of them together.

He nuzzled against her neck as they began to move to the music drifting through his apartment, and she breathed in his fresh cotton scent.

"Do you have to go back tonight?" he whispered.

Micah shook her head. She couldn't imagine leaving his arms at this moment even if a storm truck tried to drag her away. Amidst the chaos that was the wild world, here, with him, everything seemed right. This was her safe place, and though she knew she couldn't stay forever, she would soak in every second she could.

"No, I'm so tired, I don't know if I could even make it back." She hugged him closer, resting her head against his bare shoulder, his reassuring heartbeat thumping against her cheek.

"That's too bad," Lowell teased, still swaying her to the music. "I guess you'll just have to stay here, then."

Micah matched his mischievous grin with her own, and looked pointedly at his tiny apartment, lacing her words with innocence. "But there's only one bed."

Lowell shook his head in mock exasperation. "Alas. Whatever shall we do?" With that, he scooped her into his arms, a delighted squeal erupting from Micah as he threw her onto the bed. "Scoot over."

Still giggling, Micah twined herself around him as he slid in next to her. "I think we fit just right."

"Me too," Lowell said, pressing a kiss to her brow.

Micah thought of the death threats, of Calderon's mysterious murder, and the apprehension in Foster's shell-shocked expression after the will reading. "Do you really think everything will be okay?"

For a moment, Lowell was quiet, his hands stroking over her back. "With you next to me, I always feel like everything will be okay."

Micah wasn't sure how long they lay there together, feeling safe and warm under the blanket of darkness. But when she fell asleep with Lowell's warm chest pressed against her cheek, a smile still lingered on her lips.

MICAH'S INTO THE CHURN SERIES TIMELINE

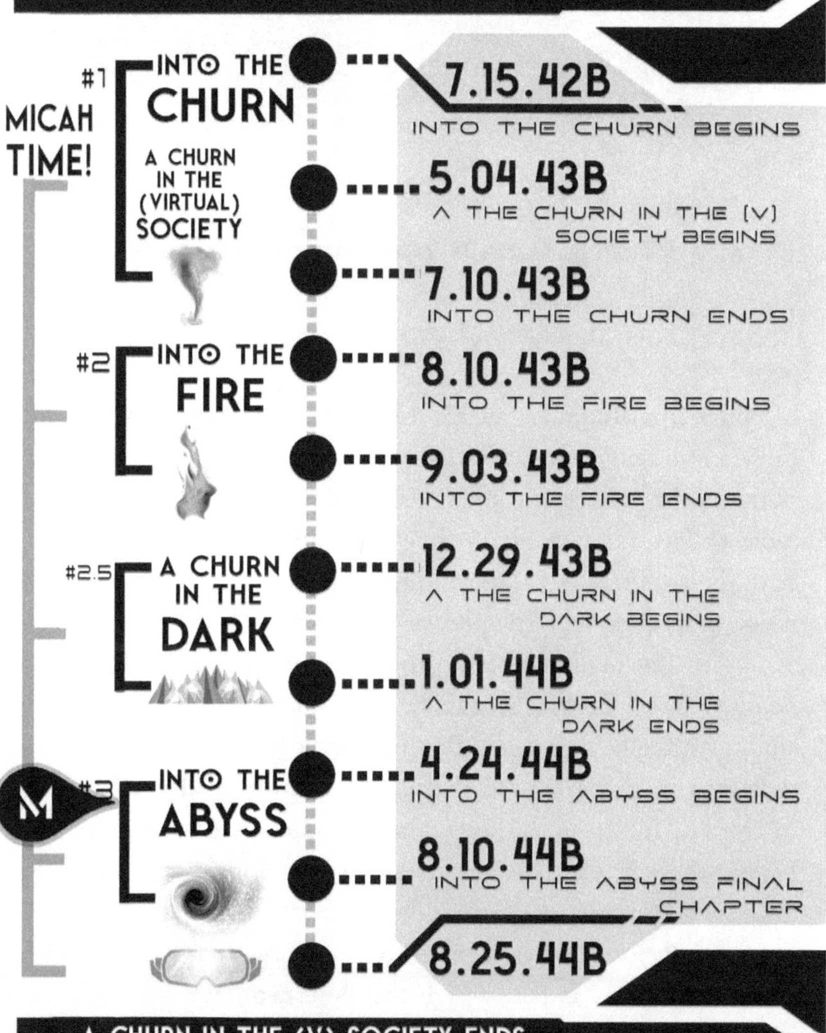

5.02.44B T-minus 2 days until the BRR

Lowell

LOWELL TUGGED at his tie and straightened his vest, internally raging against Belethea's ridiculous style customs for perhaps the millionth time. Beside him, his brothers seemed more or less comfortable in their own suits while Flora played with the ruffles of her skirt, and he couldn't help but think how much more practical the spacers' jumpsuits were.

With the madness of the upcoming BRR and Calderon's death, Lowell hadn't broached the topic of Micah with his siblings since he'd dropped the news over lunch. Which meant that, now, with the four of them wedged in their allotted space in front of the stage as they waited for the press conference to begin, the air was decidedly awkward, and they still had another fifteen minutes before the start.

Luckily Joss always seemed to know how to fill an uncomfortable silence. "Is this where the Belethean Royalers tell us they offed Calderon in a revenge scheme?"

"Don't even joke about that," Flora said, bending to glare

around Lowell. "If this is an actual murder, your misinformation could hinder a police investigation."

Joss sighed from Roland's far side. "*Joking*, Flora. Can someone please lend her a sense of humor?" He raised an eyebrow at her, his curls falling over his red goggs. "Maybe you should get a boyfriend too, Flora. It certainly seems to have relaxed Lowell."

"Am I relaxed?" Lowell rolled his unfailingly tense shoulders, all too aware of what was about to happen here—and it would change *everything*. Not only that, but this could very well be his last press conference as part of *The Royaler Review*. While he'd made the decision almost immediately after Roland's ultimatum, he hadn't quite found the words to tell his siblings just yet, and the dread of it eddied in his gut.

"I think everyone has been a little tense this week." Roland retied his long hair back away from his face, defiant curls springing free in three different directions. "But you know, after you told us about your girlfriend, I suddenly realized why you've been so happy this past year. I originally thought it was because we'd expanded the *Review*, but now I get it was probably her."

"It's both." Conflicting emotions tugged at Lowell's chest. "They're both important to me."

"And I want both you and Joss to know that you're important to me as well," Roland said. "Even if we don't share *The Royaler Review*, that doesn't mean we can't be a part of each other's lives." He shifted his weight, his lips twitching beneath his beard. "And you know... you don't have to do *The Royaler Review* just for me. Joss is finally writing what he wants; Flora, there are so many hologs that would probably die to have you; and Lowell, you're now our most successful hologger. With your ties to Sterling/Hart, you could break off with your own successful platform."

"Is this where you kick us all out?" Flora asked with a wry grin.

"No." Roland frowned, rubbing at his broad forehead. "I just... I don't want you to feel like you have to be a part of my brand. You're all amazing reporters and could do whatever you want."

"Chaff, Roland, you're always so sappy." Joss put an arm around him. "We all know that."

"Yeah." Lowell's lips quirked in a bittersweet smile, realizing there would be no better time than this moment to share the plans that had been rolling around in his mind since his confession. "I think *The Royaler Review* means a lot to all of us... which is why after this BRR, I'm going to step away to build my own brand. And that way *The Royaler Review* can keep growing without me as a complication."

"Can't say I'm surprised to hear that." Roland squeezed Lowell's shoulder. "But you'll do really well wherever you go. What about you, Flora?"

"Sorry, Roland, but you're stuck with me." Flora thrust her chin in the air and shook her head. "And even though Lowell and Joss aren't part of the *Review* anymore, don't think that means you're done with us either. I expect to see the both of you as much as humanly possible."

Joss grinned. "Aw, do you miss me already?"

"Less by the second." Flora brushed an invisible piece of dust from her puffed sleeve. "But at the end of the day, with or without *The Royaler Review*, we're family." She gently punched Joss's arm, a playful smile taking them all in. "No matter how obnoxious you all are."

Flora's words cut through the band of tension that had been squeezing Lowell's chest since the moment Joss had walked out. Because his sister was right—they'd been family before *The*

Royaler Review, and they would certainly be family after. No matter what happened.

The five-minute warning chimed in their goggs, and Micah peeked out of the side stage, her hair in an uncharacteristic brown bun. Her gaze wandered the crowd for only a minute before finding his and favoring him with a smile.

Micah: Don't you look dashing?

Lowell reflected her grin, and the rightness of his decision swelled in his chest. In the last few days, her schedule had been so busy he'd barely gotten to see her, and he knew it would only be more of the same until the end of the BRR. But afterward, when he resigned from *The Royaler Review*...? Possibilities rampaged through his thoughts.

Lowell: Well you know I dress up just for you.

His attention caught on the ambassador's coat she was wearing, and he realized with a start, she was dressed exactly like Ezren Hart.

Lowell: Wait a minute, what are you doing?

She peeked out again from the stage steps not fifteen feet from him, and mischief sparked in her smile. Beside her, a troop of event security ran up the stairs. Something was definitely going on.

Micah: Can't say. It's top secret.

Suddenly Calderon's death, and Foster's rise into his shoes took on a whole different weight. The sharp memory of the expo bombing last year stabbed into him, and before he knew what he was doing, Lowell ran toward the steps.

"Be right back," he called to his siblings as he rounded the side of the stage, flashing his press badge at security.

A solid man with a lime-green buzzcut moved to stop him, but Micah strode from the curtain's shadows toward them. "It's okay, Emmett, I know him. He's with *The Royaler Review*."

Emmett nodded but stayed close as Micah widened her

eyes in warning, her gaze darting to others in Belethean teal looking in her direction. "Can I help you?"

He leaned in next to her ear. "I don't know what you're doing, but please tell me you'll be careful."

"I'm always careful." Micah's eyes darted to Sterling/Hart hovering in the other wing and then Coach Sylvia Long talking to Simon Grady. "You don't worry about that, and we'll talk after."

A two-minute warning blared in his goggs, and Emmett's stare bored into him. Lowell's jaw tightened, resisting the urge to kiss her as he walked away.

LOWELL: EXTRA CAREFUL, MICAH. PLEASE.

MICAH: SO UNDER CONTROL! I PROMISE.

With that, he jogged back down to the side of the stage where his siblings waited.

Flora cocked an eyebrow. "What was that about?"

Lowell shook his head, the dread roaring back in full force, but this time about something completely different. The screams and shattering of the expo explosion rattled in his ears. That first terror attack was bad enough, but at least he hadn't had to worry about Micah being *onstage*. And dressed like Ezren Hart? "I just... have a bad feeling."

Joss's jaw dropped. "Wait just a fodding second. You know what they're about to announce, don't you?'

Lowell's lips tilted up. "I might have a guess."

Shock and something like admiration crossed Joss's features as he turned to Flora and Roland. "Did he tell you about this?"

"We don't have the details, but yes, he told us that he knew," Flora replied.

Joss crossed his arms with a shake of his head. "Chaff, I can't believe you're going to let him leave when he's your fritzing *in* with the biggest names in the system."

"Did I just hear you give an actual compliment to Sterling/Hart?" Roland asked with mock astonishment.

Joss shrugged, feigning indifference. "I give props where props are deserved, that's all. I have accepted, on a personal level, that they won last year, and even I can see the place is less of a shaft hole since they've been on the council." He grinned. "But Obrone is still way better, kin. See the light already."

Lowell laughed along with his siblings, each of them sharing a knowing look. Joss was obnoxious, but he was still theirs—even if he was living on Obrone now.

Joss: I WANT YOU TO KNOW, I AM HAPPY FOR YOU, LO. AND I'M SORRY I WAS SUCH AN ASSCHAFF ABOUT YOUR GIRLFRIEND BEFORE.

Lowell met his gaze, and an unseen weight lifted off his shoulders.

Lowell: THANKS, JOSS. I'M HAPPY FOR YOU TOO, KIN. I THINK WE'VE BOTH ENDED UP WHERE WE'RE SUPPOSED TO BE.

Roland opened his mouth to say something but was cut off when Foster Sterling and Ezren Hart took the stage.

With Micah's insider tips, nothing that Foster said about taking up the CEO mantle to the biggest industry in the 'verse was surprising, but Lowell still reveled in the shock of those around them. As the words left Foster's lips, Lowell fired off the articles he'd prewritten for Flora and Roland to publish, but he waited for the very end to send his own reaction into VSoc. His goggs practically blew up with messages and comms because of course, in this industry, being first meant just about everything. And Joss was right, Micah had given him that edge.

With his speech finished, Foster whirled offstage, and the hologgers surged toward the exits in an attempt to catch him. As his siblings joined the crowd, Lowell thought out a message to Micah.

Lowell: Where can I meet you?

Micah: Still top secret! I'm on a job, but I'll let you know when we're done.

Lowell's stomach sank. With the talk of the Crow and top syndicates, he knew full well that security was tight for a reason. And somehow, Micah was involved. But at this point, there was nothing he could really do about it. So instead, he did the work he was there to do.

The next four hours flew by in a blur as Lowell moved quickly to get reactions from the notable royaler VIPs in the area. Somehow luck was with him as he found Greta Sterling first in a supportive interview he knew would go viral. Next, he grabbed the Dreitis Royale Coach, who while somewhat more subdued, also had a positive reaction to the news. As the optimistic reactions poured in, Lowell swelled with hope, because he'd been right. People were seeing this as a new page turned—one without the shadow of the syndicates looming over them—and he got to spread the message to the 'verse.

It was well after midnight when Lowell finally emerged from the press conference into Petraskis's cool dome air, the thrill of a good day's work behind him, and the long list of so much left to do filling his mind. But all of that would keep until tomorrow. He couldn't wait to show Micah the breadth of the articles and perspectives they'd covered in such a short time.

He checked Micah's VSoc, only to find that oddly, she hadn't posted anything since her original reaction immediately after Foster's speech.

Lowell: Hey, when are you free to meet up?

Micah: I... I can't.

Lowell stopped dead in the middle of the street.

Lowell: What do you mean? What's wrong?

Micah: Something awful's happened, and everything is completely chaffed.

Lowell's pulse raced—adrenaline zinging along his spine. He wanted to run to her right this second, but he couldn't because he had no idea where she chaffing was. Suns, he should've followed her immediately after the press conference. Why didn't he?

Lowell: What's happened? Where are you?

Micah: I really can't even say. I'm sorry, Lo. My comms may be intermittent for a while, so just... stay safe. Please stay safe.

Lowell: Wait, are you okay?

But instead of a reply, an away message chimed in his goggs.

Micah: Hey, Belroy boys and babes! Something came up, so I won't be available for the next few days. Please enjoy the BRR hype for me, and I'll get back to you as soon as I can.

Lowell leaned against the wall, nausea rolling through his stomach. *Something came up*. Had his brother outed them even after their truce? He combed through Joss's VSoc feed, but it was all business—most of it relating to how the news drop might affect the BRR royalers' performance and what it would mean for the winners. There was some normal fritz dropped toward Belethea on the topic of favoritism, but it was nothing out of the ordinary, and Jabari, Belethea's other star hologger, had responded in kind with his own snark.

A bone-eating worry snaked through him as he checked the VSoc of the other members of the Belethean Royale team. Everything there looked strangely as expected. Sylvia, Gunderson, and Grady were all posting nonstop. And even though Sterling and Hart's VSoc accounts were run almost exclusively by Sylvia Long, they had statements posted as well.

Which left only Micah strangely silent.

He staggered onto a nearby bench for the magtrain, his legs

too weak beneath him as he mentally ran through the night's events. She'd seemed completely fine when he'd seen her backstage. So whatever happened must've occurred between then and now.

But what?

He reread her comms, looking for clues that weren't there, the last message lodged in his mind. She'd never asked him to stay safe before... so did that mean she was in danger? His hands started to tremble as he sent a quick message to Flora to contact him. There had to be hovercam footage of them leaving the press conference that could offer some answers.

A syndicate kingpin, a murder, and now this.

Suns, he was going to be sick.

Instead he ran over her last words to him again and again in his mind, but the more he read them, the more they felt like a goodbye.

5.03.44B

Lowell: Micah... I saw what happened.
Micah: You can't post it, Lowell!
Lowell: I know, the CIF already confiscated the footage, but I'm worried out of my mind. You were hurt, and they took Foster, and the security guard...
Micah: Yeah...
Lowell: This has to do with the syndicates, doesn't it? Please tell me the Crow isn't involved.
Micah: I'm all right, but I can't tell you where I am or what's going on. Honestly, I'm worried out of my mind too.
Lowell: That does not make me feel better.
Micah: I know.

5.04.44B

Lowell: The abduction news is about to drop if you don't do something. There's a guy trying to sell the footage.

Micah: Thanks, Lo. Shiro says he'll take care of it. Try to keep it as under wraps as you can.

Lowell: This feels like it's getting worse all the time.

Micah: ...Yeah...

Lowell: Please come home to me.

Micah: I'm trying.

5.04.44B

Micah: So we need serious help getting the Crow's name all over VSoc in about eleven hours. We have the bounty information from the CIF, and we need it to blow across the 'verse. Can *The Royaler Review* help us out?

Lowell: Why eleven hours?

Micah: I'm sorry, but I can't tell you.

Lowell: Flora and Roland are in, and we have other contacts that we can ask to spread the word.

Micah: Thank you—this is more important than you know.

Lowell: Anything for you, Belgirl. You know that.

5.06.44B

Lowell: Hey, just wanted to let you know I'm on my way to the finish line, but they're having some comms issues so I might be out of touch.
Lowell: Micah?
Lowell: Answer me back when you get this, I'm starting to fritz out.
Lowell: Fodding shaft it. If those syndicate asschaffs have so much as touched you, I will burn them all to the ground.
Lowell: Please be okay.
Lowell: Please.

MICAH'S **INTO THE CHURN** SERIES

TIMELINE

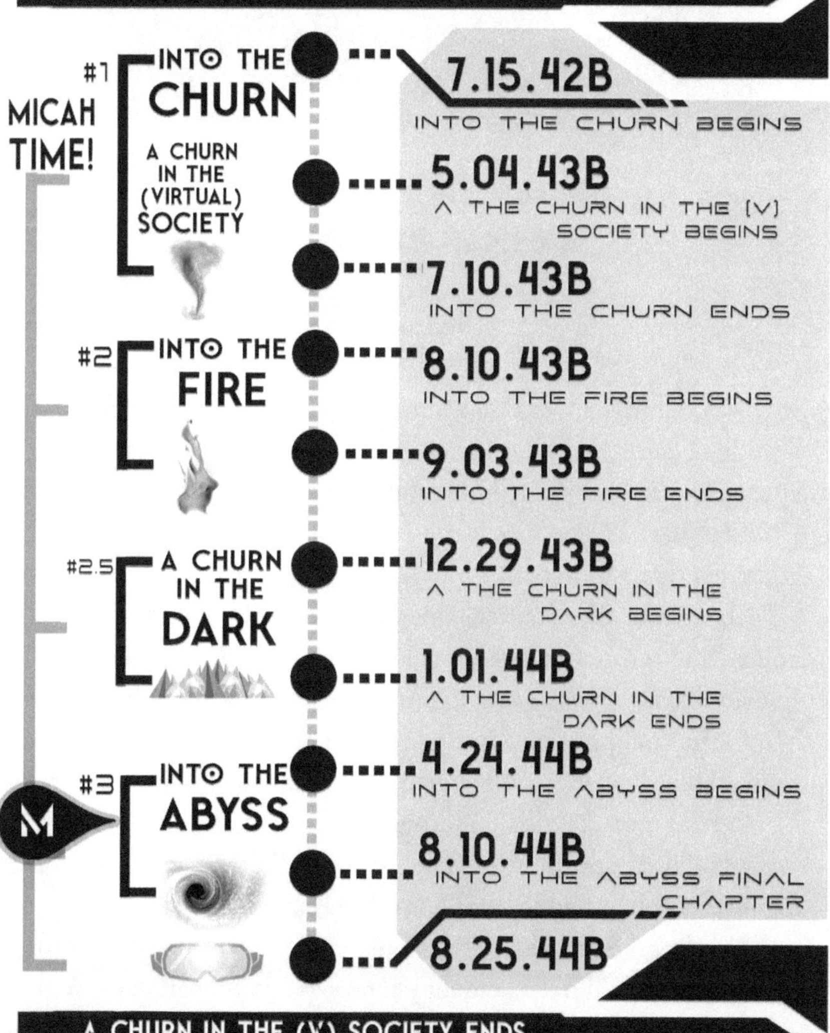

5.08.44B BRR Day 5

Micah

MICAH'S HEART rattled against her ribs as the ship jerked to a sudden stop on the runway. Connecting her goggs to the spaceport's network, she immediately sent a message to Lowell.

Micah: There's a bomb at the finish line—you have to get everyone to evacuate!

She sent an identical message to Sylvia and silently counted to ten before she let cold acceptance sink to the pit of her stomach. Someone was jamming the finish line's comms.

In the cockpit, Shiro turned and pointed a finger directly at Sam. "You. Stay. Here. Or so help me, I will arrest you."

"We're not fodding kidding, Sam," Micah added as she wriggled into one of the spare topsuits they kept on board. Unfortunately it had to be at least three sizes too big.

"It's fine," Sam said, feigning nonchalance even as his teeth chattered. "You'll need someone who's got comms when you're at the finish, and I'll try to break through the jamming block remotely."

"Good thought." Shiro gripped his shoulder with a glance down at Waffle and Turnip at their feet. "And if anything happens, take care of my cat."

"But nothing's going to happen." Micah wrapped Sam in a brief squeeze. "We'll see you when we get back."

Shiro turned to her as he strapped a myriad of weapons to his torso. "Are you sure you want to come? You can stay too."

"No." Micah shook her head, even as a flurry of panic accelerated her pulse. "You'll need someone to manually hack into the trains on site, and I have more data on these storms than anyone, even if they're going off the charts."

Shiro nodded, picking up his tactical topsuit helmet and tossing one to her—also too big. "All right, let's go then."

With that, Shiro ran toward the docking ramp and through the teeming hangar while Micah raced to keep up, unused to the topsuit's drain on her body. He projected his CIF agent credentials in front of him as he shouldered through the crowd to the adjacent magtrain station. "Clear out! Civilian transits to the BRR finish line are no longer authorized." Shiro's goggs projected his voice, and his message echoed again through everyone's chips in a mass statement from the CIF.

The din of chaos only swelled as the crowd parted before him, and Micah tried to pin herself to his shadow. The spaceport's security moved to hold the masses of BRR fans back while some of them shouted her name, but Micah had no bandwidth to do anything but focus on her wheezing lungs. Her legs burning, she and Shiro jumped onto the platform just as a train pulled into the station.

They waited only a moment for the passengers to trickle out before they rushed on and the doors slid shut behind them. Micah propped her hands on her knees, dragging in lungfuls of air while Shiro commandeered the train's controls. She'd just collapsed into a seat when the underground train took off again towards the finish line. With sweat already stinging her eyes, Micah wrenched off the topsuit helmet, mentally pulling up every hologger she knew to try to get the word out about the terrorist threat.

But while she worked, all she could think about was getting to the finish line. Of Ezren and Foster jumping out into the storm. Of the blood the Crow had already spilled on Janusoth Station. Of the royalers fighting through the super-charged churn just to get to a finish line primed to kill them. And everyone else she cared about.

The panic screaming through her was almost deafening.

And even though she knew the comms were jammed, she couldn't resist trying to send a message to Lowell just in case.

Micah: We're on our way to the finish line to get the trains moving.

Micah: Try to find Ezren and Foster—they're going to need help to find the bomb.

She wanted to tell him to get out of there, but with the trains stuck and the killer storms raging outside, there was nowhere for him—or anyone else—to go. Shiro stood beside her, his own official CIF holo glowing as they tried to come up with alternate plans.

In her goggs, the storm built in intensity to record-breaking levels, sending the VSoc terraformers into their own frenzy. She watched the royalers struggle against the storm, maydays going off left and right. And Sterling/Hart, Grady/Guns, and the Amarals were all somewhere out in that? The thought made her want to vomit.

"Shiro, what if Ezren and Foster don't make it through the storm?" Micah whispered.

"Then it'll be up to us to find the bomb and disable it," Shiro said, his hard voice brooking no room for argument.

"But what if we don't get there in time?"

Shiro turned to her then, his dark eyes softening only slightly. "Micah, stay away from the what-ifs. We can only deal with the situation directly in front of us. If we do anything else, we're wasting precious time."

Micah drew her knees to her chest and wrapped her arms around them, every worst-case scenario barreling through her head, and through it all, one thought stopped her cold. She hadn't told Lowell she loved him. She knew without asking they'd both been waiting for the day they wouldn't have to hide behind a secret. But what a ridiculous notion that seemed now.

She'd been so caught up with VSoc and her new job, when she could've been spending time with him. Instead, they saw each other only in stolen moments, worried about an image that now seemed so ridiculously inane. But it had always seemed like they would have more time later. When things weren't so busy. Weren't so crazy. When they wouldn't have to be a secret any longer...

And now absolutely none of that mattered.

How stupid she'd been.

"I feel like we're already out of time, and there are so many things I should've said. Should've done." Her voice was barely a whisper. "Why didn't I?"

Shiro's shoulders fell. "Because we don't expect heinous things to happen. You did your best with life as you knew it, and there's nothing wrong with that. And now, we have to do our best to make sure we still have that tomorrow left to live."

A tear streaked down Micah's cheek, and she swiped it away. Because of course he was right. If she wanted to cling to any hope at all, she had to focus. Blocking out the other distractions, Micah worked with Sam as they tried to crack the comms jam again and again in a dozen different ways. Still, time raced by with the train hurtling towards the storm of the millennia. With their friends' lives hanging in the balance.

When the train gave them a two-minute arrival warning, Micah shot to her feet, fresh adrenaline slamming into her chest. "We're here! I've got to find Lowell."

"No." Shiro's face hardened into the calculating mask of a CIF officer—not at all Sylvia's jovial fiancé in this moment. "I know you want to make sure he's safe, just like I want to find Sylvia. But if we want to help them, first you need to get those trains running. Don't forget why we're here." He held her gaze. "We have to help them all."

Suddenly the lives of thousands of people seemed to drop on Micah's shoulders all at once. "But I'm just a fangirl hologger, Shiro. I don't know if I can..."

"You are not *just* anything, Micah," Shiro said. "You care about this race more than anyone I know, you work miracle-level science, and you always find solutions where no one else can. You change people's minds and you make things happen—and today, you're going to do it again to save their lives."

Micah straightened, taking deep breaths under his stare. She thought of Ezren running into the storms again and again. Risking her life over and over. Of her and Foster's speeches about change. About one step at a time. Of the impossible odds that royalers faced. Of the impossible problems Belethea had solved to terraform an untamable planet.

All the things she preached. Of the impact she yearned for.

Things Micah truly believed in.

And the truth was, she didn't have to solve the whole problem, because she was a part of a team she could count on. A team that was counting on her to solve her piece of this puzzle. She took one last deep breath. "Okay, I'm ready."

With that, the train screeched to a stop, and they raced out into the chaos.

MICAH'S INTO THE CHURN SERIES
TIMELINE

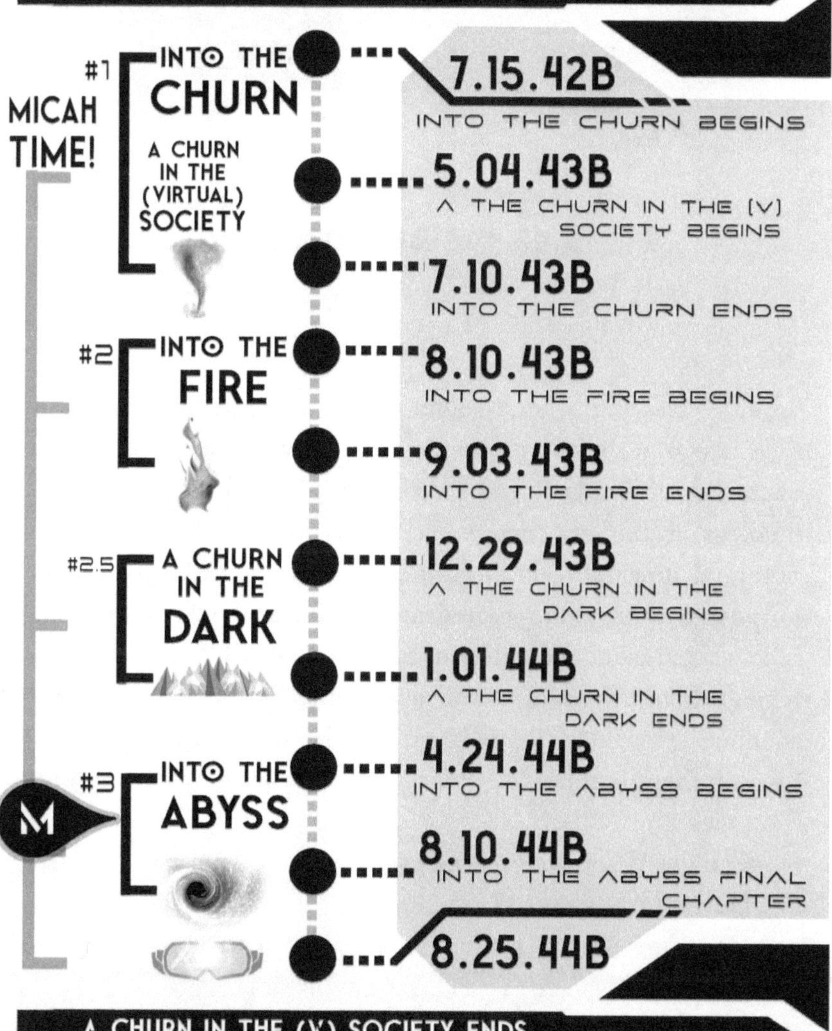

5.08.44B BRR Day 5

Lowell

CRAMMED into a side room with a dozen other panicked race personnel while the walls quaked with the force of the exponentially intensifying death storm, Lowell focused on his hologs as he sent Ezren everything he'd gathered on the potential terrorist. Somewhere in the basement levels of the outpost, Sterling/Hart rooted around for a bomb threatening to blow everyone to a distant star, and all he could do was funnel them information and hope Micah's complete faith in them was justified. Meanwhile, in the background of his goggs, his siblings bombarded him with completely unhelpful messages

Flora: We just got on the train. Where are you?

Lowell: I'm safe. Just go.

Roland: You'd better not be doing this to get the eyewitness story—it's not worth it.

Lowell: You don't have to worry. It's really not about that.

Joss: LOWELL, GET YOUR ASS ON THE TRAIN! DO NOT MAKE ME COME GET YOU.

Lowell: Don't you dare. You'll only put us all in more danger.

Joss: I know I said I was cool with your Belethea coverage, but if they're asking you to do this, I WILL KILL THEM.

Lowell: It's not about the coverage, Joss. We're trying to save lives. Now, I'm sorry, but I have to go.

While his siblings had managed to get on the first train moving out, there were still so many people left in the outpost, there was no way they'd be able to evacuate them all in time. Somewhere the storm dirge played for another dead royaler, and Lowell winced.

Ezren: Okay, thanks, Lowell. Also, Micah's coming to you. Make sure you keep her safe.

Lowell nearly jumped off his seat on the floor, the panic he'd been shoving down threatening to knot his throat.

Lowell: What?!!? I told her specifically *NOT* to come. I've been fritzing out for the past three days thinking she was dead and now... Just WHY.

He raked a hand through his curls, forcing himself to calm as he slid back down the walls. Hysteria wouldn't help anything right now.

Lowell: No, it's fine. It'll be fine. I'll find her. Thanks, Ezren.

A scream punctuated the howling wind from the exposed atrium of the finish line along with the whining shriek of bending metal. Suns, Micah better be on the lower levels somewhere.

Lowell: Micah, are you at the finish line!? Where are you!?

Lowell leaned his head back against the wall, the storm

roaring in his ears while Coach Sylvia Long crossed her arms from where she sat beside him. "I still don't know about you. How do you know Ezren?" Her voice barely carried over the screaming wind while Coach Greta Sterling, clad in a silver topsuit, tried to keep the injured calm in the center of the room. All gazes held rapt to the holos coating the walls of royalers balancing on the brink of death.

"I don't really know Ezren, but..." He bit down on the inside of his cheek, the worry that had been threatening to strangle him coming to the surface. "Have you heard from Micah?"

Sylvia's gaze sharpened. "How do you know Micah? I'm not sure where she is."

"Ezren just said she was here."

"Here?!" Sylvia's voice pitched, echoing his own terror, before she remembered to lower it again, confusion wrinkling her brow. "But why would Ezren tell you that?"

Lowell sighed again, and his hair whipped in the wind leaking in the cracked door, lashing at his eyes. With people dying around them and their own death staring them in the face, he didn't have the energy to lie anymore. In this moment, images and brands were just words, and he only had the truth left. "Because I'm in love with your VSoc manager."

For a stretched moment, Sylvia only stared at him. Uncertainty crawled up his collar as he shifted on the hard floor, and he was about to open his mouth again when a surprised laugh bubbled out of her. "Is this why *The Royaler Review* has been taking it easy on us?"

"We don't take it easy on anyone," Lowell said in an almost automatic response. "But our platform has shifted away from critique to a more equally supportive publication."

Sylvia snorted, something about the stress in the lines of her face making her slight smile seem borderline unhinged. "And how long has this been going on?"

"A little under a year, I guess."

Sylvia shook her head, a blend of confused disbelief quirking her words. "Why didn't you tell anyone?"

Now it was Lowell's turn to chuckle. "Well, with the history of enmity between her platform and mine, we were a little concerned about how our bosses would react." He gave her a pointed glance, and a distant scream echoed from the atrium.

Sylvia's rainbow brows knitted as her gaze drifted to the holopro where Grady/Guns fought for their lives. "Okay, maybe there was a time when I wouldn't have taken the news so well. But in the light of actual problems, I hope the two of you are happy together."

It was such a matter-of-fact statement, Lowell's mouth twisted in a humorless grin. "I guess announcements are all about timing."

Agent Shiro Tanaka: This is an official evacuation order from the CIF. The trains are now running. Everyone proceed to boarding level B3.

"Micah's probably with Shiro," Sylvia said, the shuddering of the walls punctuated with violent cracks. "But there's no way we can make it to the stairs in this."

Lowell watched as the debris whipped through the ruined atrium at terrifying speed. He didn't know how many people—or bodies—had already been stolen away by the winds, but they would certainly be next if they tried to run across the four hundred yards of open space to the stairwell. The crack widened in the door, and the howl of the wind pitched to a scream.

Lowell: We can't stay here either though. When that bomb explodes, we're dead.

A spidery crack spread through the ceiling, and as one, they followed its trajectory from one wall to the other.

Lowell: *If* this room lasts that long.

Sylvia: I can't leave my royalers. Simon and Bex are only a handful of miles away.

Lowell: And they stand a better chance of surviving in their topsuits than you do in those heeled boots.

Sylvia glanced down at her heels as if considering her VSoc-ready ruffles and lace for the first time.

Sylvia: Fair.

"Okay, everyone," Greta boomed, her voice resonating with authority. "If you're taking a shot at the stairwell make sure you hug the wall." She moved toward the door with decisive steps, her topsuit granting her an advantage that the rest of them decidedly lacked.

Lowell was still turning the choices over in his mind when Micah finally answered his message.

Micah: We got the trains running! Where are you? Are you okay?!

Lowell: I'm fine. Sylvia, Greta Sterling, and I are in a small room off the atrium.

A massive piece of debris crashed into the glass wall, shattering it. With piercing shrieks, everyone in the room turned away from the flying glass. Lowell nearly choked on his thrashing heart, the wind now bellowing through the room, threatening to snatch them out.

Lowell: You need to get on one of those trains and get away from here.

Micah: We're not leaving without you. The storm's only getting stronger. *Everyone* needs to get out.

Lowell: Okay, we will. Just stay where you are.

"We have to leave!" Lowell yelled over the cacophony of whistling air as he pulled Sylvia to her feet.

Greta waved toward the stairwell. "We'll all go together. Stay low and close." With that, she led the dozen refugees out into the storm, sliding along the wall as they shuffled through the tearing gale. Lowell sucked in a deep breath, trying to calm his flipping stomach. Well, if he was going out in this, he might as well let *The Royaler Review* benefit from his last moments. He turned on his goggs cam and posted a quick message.

THE ROYALER REVIEW: LIVE FROM THE FINISH LINE ATRIUM RAVAGED BY THE STORM—SURVIVORS STRUGGLE TO MAKE IT TO SAFETY. WARNING, EXTREME AND UNPREDICTABLE CIRCUMSTANCES MAY LEAD TO GRAPHIC IMAGES.

That done, Lowell followed after the others, holding his arms up to protect his head from the shards of rubble and stone flying through the air. He looked up to see uncountable funnel clouds twisting through the murderous sky, just waiting for a place to land, and he broke out in a cold sweat. While his magboots' strength was at full power, he could feel them wavering beneath the force of the sharp gusts.

They were making solid progress when a wind-blasted sheet of metal ricocheted off the wall. The line in front of him scattered as people dove for cover, and the debris bounced off the wall again with a horrific smash. Lowell slid to his stomach, shielding his head from another shower of debris, but when he looked up once more, at least half of their party were nowhere to be seen. Distantly, he was aware of the storm dirge playing again in the background of his goggs and ahead of him, Sylvia screamed.

His gaze flitted to the names popping up in his goggs: Kit and Dean Amaral.

Deceased.

"Holy shaft," he breathed, heart pounding out of his chest

and rain pouring into his eyes. With the nightmare around him, he could barely process the reality of what he was seeing. In the diminished oxygen of the churn belt, his breathing came in short gasps and he realized if he didn't get to the stairwell or find a topsuit soon, he would black out.

And they didn't bother playing the dirge for hologgers.

He flinched as something hard scraped across his back, and crawled toward where Greta, protected in her suit, shielded Sylvia against the wall not far from the stairwell. But they still seemed so far away.

Micah: A complex tornado system is about to touch down in the atrium. We're talking multiple funnels supercharged with debris. LOWELL. GET OUT NOW. The survival rate is plummeting!

Lowell looked back at the bestial atmosphere where the funnel clouds wove ever closer.

Lowell: I think you're right.

Micah: Wait, I see your feed on VSoc. Mother fodding suns, Lowell, you can't stand still, you have to keep moving!

Lowell's stomach sank as he wedged himself into a dent in the wall, heaving in shallow breaths. There was no way he was going to make it to the stairwell.

Lowell: Micah... I love you. I should've told you a million times.

Micah: LOWELL, STOP. I'm coming to get you.

Lowell: No, don't!

He'd barely gotten the message out before a figure in a full tactical topsuit burst through the stairwell door. He took one swift glance before sprinting off at unnatural speed toward Sylvia and Greta.

Lowell tried to move toward them when a metal rod impaled itself into the wall next to his head. *Holy chaff.* He'd barely flinched back when another figure in a baggy topsuit skidded through the stairwell door and straight into the heart of the storm. She didn't make it four steps before a rock crashed into her helmet, knocking her to the ground. The helmet flew off her head and into the wind as she skidded along the floor. With the maelstrom whipping her teal pigtails free of their bindings, she staggered to her feet, her gaze tearing across the wreckage of the finish line.

"MICAH!" The wind snatched Lowell's voice away as he staggered to his feet.

If the guy in the tac-suit noticed her presence, he gave no sign as he swept Sylvia onto his shoulder in one easy movement and shepherded Greta through the stairwell.

Agent Shiro Tanaka: Everyone evacuate the atrium immediately—collapse is imminent.

Agent Shiro Tanaka: I repeat, EVACUATE THE ATRIUM IMMEDIATELY.

But Micah didn't move. Her searching, teal stare swung in Lowell's direction, their gazes locking for only a second.

And then the twister touched down. Right in the middle of everything.

Ears roaring and pure horror coursing through him, Lowell didn't have time to consider anything but that very second as he ran into the deadly churn after her.

MICAH'S INTO THE CHURN SERIES

TIMELINE

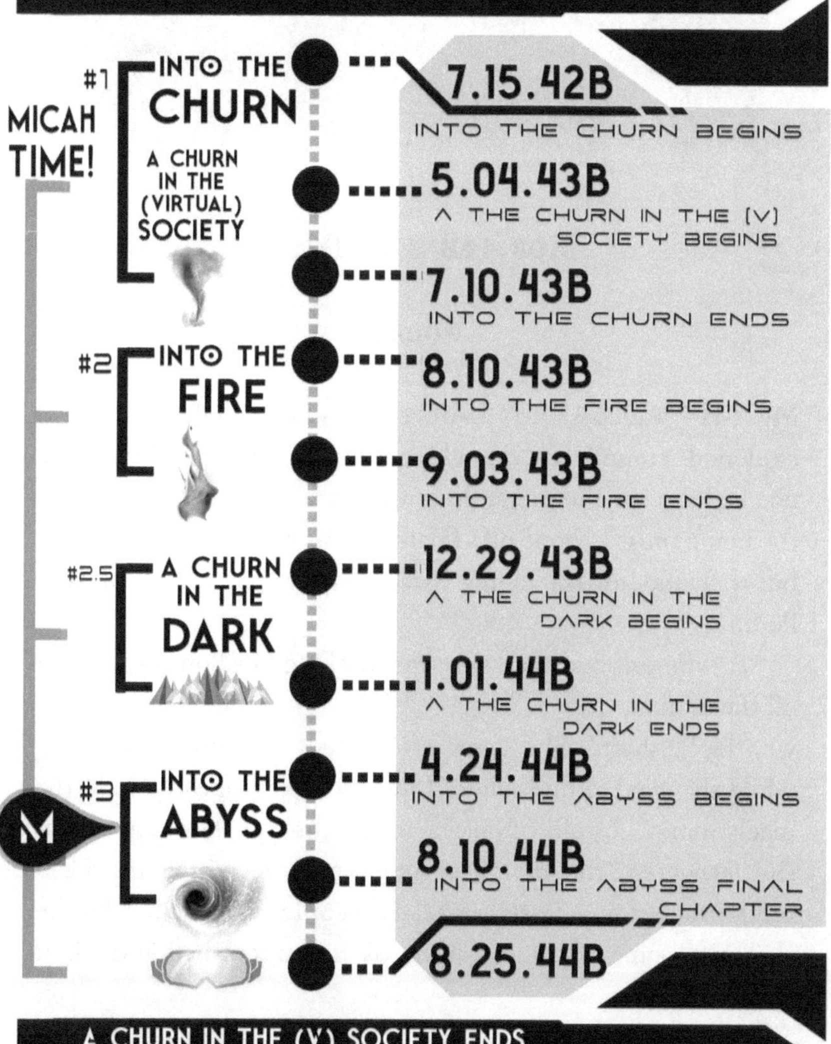

5.08.44B BRR Day 5

Micah

MICAH HAD BARELY LAID eyes on Lowell when the world exploded around her, knocking her off her feet. Her head cracked against the metal floor and for a moment, she thought the bomb must've gone off. That this was the end of all of them, but then she saw the raging twister barreling across the atrium floor.

A different end than she was thinking but honestly not far off the mark.

"Holy shaft." She leapt to her feet, her vision doubling while she tried to find where Lowell had disappeared to in the maelstrom. "Lowell!" Nausea rolled through her stomach as she staggered, the merciless wind and her throbbing head rendering her hopelessly unsteady. People raced by her for the stairwell, some of them falling as debris crashed into their bodies.

Micah: Lowell!

Lowell: Run, Micah!

But she couldn't, not when she didn't know where he was. She had to find him. Find Ezren. She was supposed to be helping Ezren, wasn't she? Why couldn't she focus? She had to —something hard banged into her shoulder and threw her to the floor. Groaning, she opened her eyes only to find the empty gaze of a lifeless body staring at her. With a shriek, she tried to scramble away from it, but her limbs weren't cooperating amidst the sucking gusts.

Agent Shiro Tanaka: Atrium structural integrity has been completely compromised. Take shelter on the lower levels. We have security in place to guide the Royale finishers to safety.

But Micah could barely parse the words, her mind frozen over with fear. She couldn't breathe, her heart hammering as terrified tears clogged her throat. She was too far from the stairwell, too far from Lowell, too far from everything.

Then the twister bashed into the side of the atrium, and with a deafening crack, the wall started to crumble. Micah raised her arms in a last attempt to protect herself as debris showered down on her. But then someone was grabbing her hands and yanking her to her feet.

"Run, Micah!" Lowell shouted, pushing her in front of him as everything fell apart behind them. "You can do it. Run!"

But she couldn't. Her balance was gone. Her oxygen depleted and her lungs burning. Her feet tripped on the first metal spar, and she pitched toward the ground. But then his hands were on her again, swinging her into his arms and shouldering into a side room. He shoved her unceremoniously under a metal table before forming a protective shell around her. His wide eyes met hers as the vortex roared past and the atrium collapsed onto the table in a shrieking crash.

"I love you, Lowell!" she yelled over the clatter, tears beading in her eyes as the debris continued to rain down. It was a world apart from the quiet, perfect moment she'd been waiting for, but sometimes things didn't have to be perfect. Relief whispered through her that she'd been lucky enough to tell him at all. "I just thought I'd get the chance to say it more."

His features softened with desperation, and his lips met hers in a fierce, unyielding kiss. Something banged into the table above them, and Lowell's mouth left hers as he tugged her into a tight embrace. "And I love you." The other side of the atrium collapsed, sending a shudder to the floor, and the table above them groaned with the weight. "Too much to let you go today. The stars will have to find someone else to light the dark."

But as they sat there waiting for the table to crush them, the seconds only continued to roll by, and the roar of the tornado abated. No world-ending explosion erased them from Belethea's surface, and still they breathed in the dust of the wreckage.

Micah checked her goggs and found, to her shock, that the storm seemed to be abating, if only slightly. "I think..." Her eyes found Lowell's. "I think we may be past the worst of the storm, but... what about the bomb?"

"I don't know." Lowell let out a shaky breath. "But suns, Micah, you scared the chaff out of me. Are you hurt?" He gingerly probed the tender spot on the back of her head, and she winced. But the small injury felt like a miracle in the spectrum of what could've been.

Micah opened her mouth to respond when the ground shuddered below them, and a distant explosion cracked through the air. Micah shrieked, and Lowell's arms wrapped protectively around her again. She screwed her eyes shut tight as she waited for the table to give out. For the pain and the darkness.

But nothing else happened.

They'd survived.

"Ezren and Foster..." Lowell whispered, his eyes shining. "They did it."

Micah let out an incredulous laugh. "Of course they did. They're my Sterling/Hart. I've always said that they could do anything." She raised a teasing brow, suppressing a wince. "You'd better be nice to them when you write about this."

Lowell tried for an affronted look that only half-succeeded. "I'm always nice."

"That must be my good influence," Micah said.

"Okay, well then, Ms. Good Influence, just this once then, I'll admit you were—"

The whine of two overlapping mayday calls cut through Micah's goggs only to be echoed by Lowell's. Micah's brow furrowed as she pulled up the notification and then her heart nearly stopped beating.

Ezren Hart.

And Foster Sterling.

No pulse detected.

Whatever was keeping Micah up seemed to give out, as she dragged in a gasp. "*No.*" Hot tears blurred her vision all over again. Not after everything Ezren and Foster had been through. Not after they'd saved everyone. She turned to Lowell, but his face had gone white, his gaze distant with his own shock. Micah shook her head, still refusing to believe it. "That can't be right," she whispered. "They can't be dead."

Wordlessly, Lowell gathered her in his arms. To his credit, he didn't say everything would be okay. He didn't hush her as the sobs racked her body. Or make a single sound as the storm dirge played its melancholy notes through their goggs. He was simply there, experiencing it right along with her, and she didn't have to look at VSoc to know that the 'verse was mourning with them.

"If they're dead, what was this all for?" Micah whispered.

Lowell was silent for a long minute before finally he answered. "It was for Casolla, Micah. All of your work, and Sterling/Hart's sacrifice... it's always been for Casolla."

Perhaps that was true, on some grand scale. But now, in this moment, even Casolla didn't seem worth it. So lost was she in her own grief, she almost didn't notice the goggs messages from Shiro.

Shiro: Micah, where are you?

Shiro: Micah, are you okay?

Shiro: Micah! Answer!!

Her face still buried in Lowell's chest, she forced herself to think out a response.

Micah: What.

Shiro: Thank the suns you're alive. I need you to get the word out that Ezren and Foster neutralized the terrorist threat, and they're alive.

"WHAT?!" Micah shrieked, straightening, and Lowell looked at her as if she were a bomb herself.

"What is it? What's wrong?"

"They're alive!" Micah screeched.

Lowell bolted up straight next to her, only to bang his head on the table with a wince. "How do you know?"

Micah: You're sure!!? You'd better not be fritzing me.

Shiro: Yes, we're in contact with Ezren and en route to pick them up. Now spread the message before every hologger on VSoc shoves out their own narrative.

Micah: On it.

Filled with fresh resolve, she turned to Lowell with a determined grin. "So, I know we're trapped under a mountain of debris, but Ezren and Foster are alive, the story is fresh, and we have work to do."

Lowell let out a laugh of disbelief, running a hand over his bruised jaw. "Well okay, then. If we have good news to report, let's get it out there."

But before Micah pulled up her VSoc, she paused, her gaze strafing the rubble around them before gripping Lowell's hands. "Lo," she said softly. "I... this is going to be messy and I don't know if it'll be the brand you'r—"

"Micah, it doesn't have to be perfect," Lowell said, squeezing her hands. "As long as we tell our truth. That's what the world needs right now."

Micah's teeth sank into her bottom lip, the truth of his words vibrating in her bones. "Then I want you to know that my truth is I don't care if anyone knows about us." In the face of everything that happened she could scarcely believe she'd ever cared about something so trivial. "I just want to be with you. Together for real. Job be chaffed."

And his grin seemed to light the shadows beneath the soft white glow of his goggs. "Oh, my love." He pressed a soft kiss to her brow and then her lips. "That's all I want too." His grin took a sheepish lilt. "So I guess you won't mind then that I already told Sylvia? She seemed okay with it," he added quickly. "And I told Roland I'm resigning from *The Royaler Review* to start my own hololog."

"Is that really what you want?" Micah asked, the rubble creaking around them. Suns, it had better not collapse on them down here when their future just now seemed to be shifting into place.

He reached out and wound her wild teal hair around his finger. "Micah, I want you. Everything else is just details." His eyes swam with earnestness, each word coated in a soft, unbearable love. "I want to be able to look toward a future where you can move into my tiny apartment with me. And I can cook for you and walk you to work every day. Where I can do my job and you can do yours and we'll take time to just be together without caring what anyone thinks."

Micah gave him a wobbling smile, happy tears starting to spill down her cheeks. "I'd love that."

And in that moment, Micah wasn't thinking of VSoc or of what came next. Of the BRR, politics, or anything else. When Lowell's soft lips met hers, it was a celebration of survival. Of a story not yet over. Their story. One that she looked forward to continuing. And one she believed in with her whole heart.

Despite their still fritzy predicament beneath a literal ton of rubble, when Lowell pulled back, his bright smile matched hers.

"Now, are you ready to spin a story?"

Her grin widened in anticipation. "I think it's time we let the 'verse know what happened here."

"Together?"

"Together."

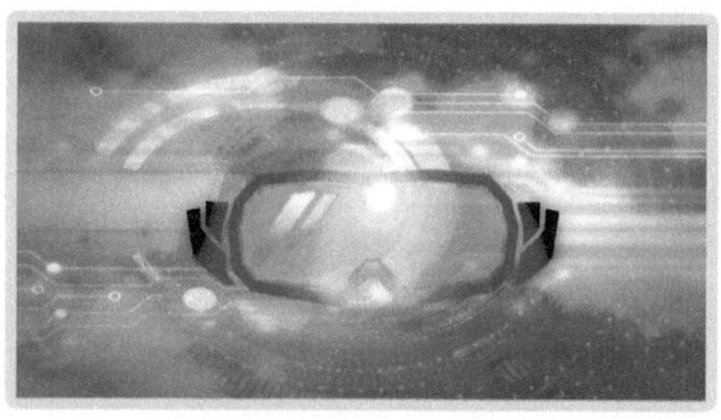

BRRflagship: Okay wait, did anyone else see *The Royaler Review* guy and Belethea's VSoc manager get crushed at the finish line?
HartlingForever: After he tried to save her life?! Broke my heart!
RunDriveFight: NOOOO!! They're the two best hologs Belethea has.
IllBeAtTheFinishLine: No! They're okay! *The Royaler Review* has announced that they're trapped beneath the rubble but alive.
DreitisTeamCaptain: Holy chaff. That has to be one in a million then. Some weren't so lucky.
StationRunner: May the stars take them home.
Legslegslegs: Okay, well if they don't get together after that, there's something not right in the world.
CrionianRoyaler: I'm here for that good news story. Suns knows we need it.
WheresMyStormTruck: Well, @BeletheanBRR and @TheRoyalerReview, that settles it. We need a follow-up story on Lowell Coppen & Micah Belanger stat!

MICAH'S **INTO THE CHURN** SERIES

TIMELINE

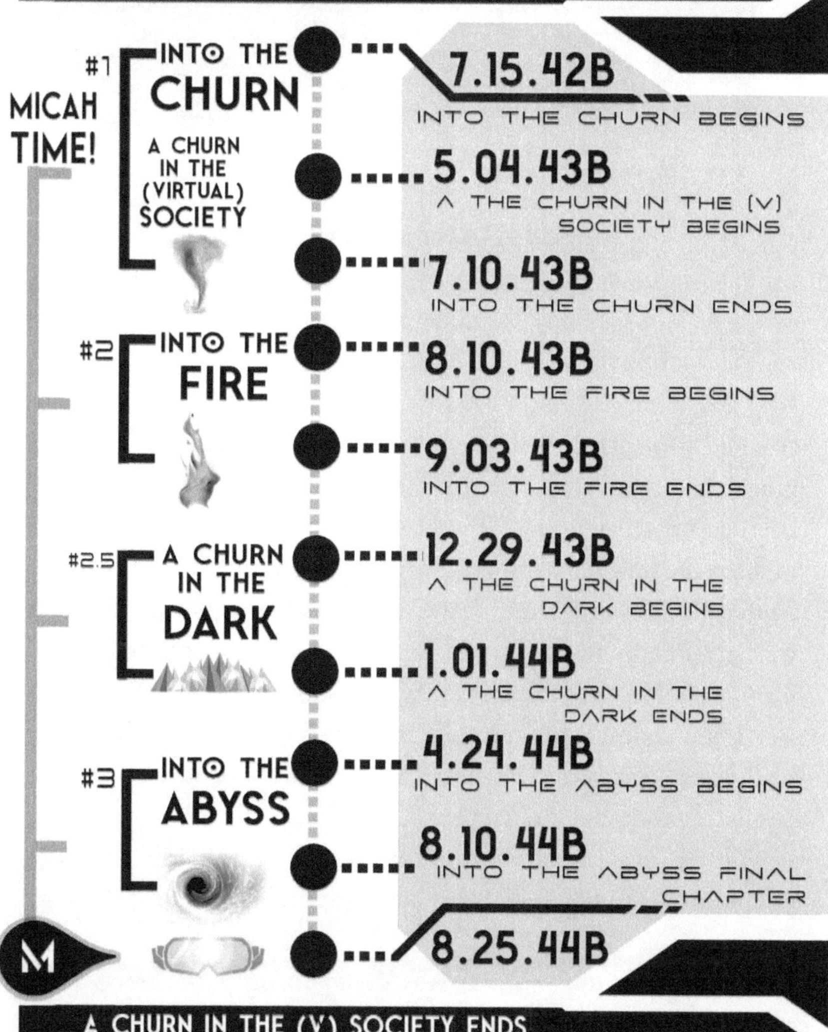

8.25.44B: Just another day

Lowell

AFTER THE HOLOS of Lowell and Micah nearly getting crushed to death tore through VSoc like a whirlwind, they no longer had to worry about announcing their relationship to the BRR community. In fact, by the time the two of them returned to Tuzuno, half of VSoc was shipping them together. While of course there were some detractors, Joss's overpowering voice was not one of them. In fact, Lowell might've even called his input quietly supportive, as crazy as it sounded.

Then again, it seemed like in some ways, the whole 'verse had been turned on its head at that BRR. But somewhere amidst the chaos and tragedy—and frantic hologging from beneath a collapsed building—VSoc loved the idea of two people brought together from opposite ends of the royale in a deadly crisis.

And absolutely no one was going to drop the news that they'd gotten together long before then.

So after Roland had practically crushed the life out of him

in a bear hug, he'd also begged him to remain with *The Royaler Review*. Now Lowell was responsible for all Sterling/Hart news and underdog stories from the bottom third teams of the BRR. Roland had even included Joss once more in *The Royaler Review* guest posts for Obrone, and they'd managed to hire on three more hologgers to cover the rest of the royale teams. Meanwhile, Flora focused on the finance and political sectors of the BRR, and the expansion that they'd always talked of was officially a reality.

So now, with Petraskis's new clear dome showing off the true Belethean sky, Lowell walked past the newly renamed Amaral Hall's front gates and through the doors into the team's bustling lobby. Three new recruits jockeyed around the refrigerator as they called out to him, while two second-year racers clapped him on the shoulder before they raced out the doors. Even though it was only the beginning of the season, the air brimmed with the excitement of a fresh start while Belethea's two championship cups looked on proudly from the corner.

Micah and Simon Grady's conversation about VSoc cred and holo numbers echoed down the stairway as they strode into the room with Bex following after them like a shadow in her new security role. Bex nodded to Lowell in acceptance while Jain and Costa, two of the new recruits, tried to goad him into an exclusive with glowing confidence and infectious laughter.

It was a moment that made Lowell himself feel like part of the team, filling him with a new appreciation for Micah's passion. Finishing her conversation, she bounded across the lobby and threw her arms around him as if he didn't pick her up from work every day. It was a short walk to their new apartment in the Navarro building across the street with the rest of the Belethean management team, but it was one they never missed no matter how busy they were.

Walking back out the door, he put his arm around her

shoulders while she described the fresh training regimen Simon and Greta, Belethea's new coaches, had mapped out. Lowell smiled and laughed along with her while she related the pranks already flying between the veteran and the rookie racers. A grin still lingered on his face as they crossed the street, and he tilted his head to catch a glimpse of Casolla through the dusky navy clouds swirling across her luminous sphere.

He stopped in the garden beside Navarro Hall, his gaze still stuck on Belethea's actual twilight sky—not a holo—glowing above them.

"What?" Micah cocked her head, following his gaze.

He shifted his attention to her. "I think if I could freeze time, I would stop it on this day."

Micah snorted. "It's a Tuesday, Lo. And if we froze today, then we'd never actually get to see next year's BRR."

"Okay," he relented, setting his hands on her waist as he faced her. "But if I could travel through the history holo to anywhere I wanted, I would still come back to today."

"And what's so special about today?" Micah asked, her pink pigtail buns glowing in the silvery light. "It was a good day, but it was kind of an ordinary good day."

"I know." His grin widened. "And on this very ordinary good day, I think I'm happier than I've ever been."

Micah burst into the oddly deep belly laugh he loved so much. "Well, if you like this, I think it only gets better from here, Viewboy."

Lowell nodded, mentally retracing his steps—all the pieces that had to come together to make that exact moment. "But what if Roland had never started *The Royaler Review* or Calderon hadn't done any of those awful things? What if Ezren Hart hadn't tried out for Belethea's Race Royale Team?"

"You think we would've passed like the ships between the stars?" Micah's arms wrapped around him, her violet eyes softening. "Brushing past each other without ever actually meeting?"

"Maybe there's a 'verse out there where we did." The thought sent a spike of anxiety through him. "So is it bad that I'm grateful things happened the way they did to bring me to you? That seems pretty horribly selfish. Even for me."

"I think..." The words rolled off of Micah's tongue, her expression thoughtful as she looked back up at Casolla's lava-scarred face. "We should grab whatever joy we have and hold on to it." She squeezed him for emphasis, a smile curving her lips.

Lowell gathered her tighter to him. "Then I might have to hold on to you forever."

"Please do," she whispered.

Lowell didn't know how long they stood out there in the quiet garden looking up at the stars, but he knew even if he lived until they all turned to stardust, he would still be holding on to that joy. The joy of a hopeful future, of the love of his life smiling in his arms, and the world coming alive around them.

Maybe he wouldn't freeze time after all.

Because with as far as they'd come, into the churn and back out, this was just the beginning.

Of their love.

Of their journey.

Of their brand-new world.

And he couldn't wait to see what mountains they would move next.

ACKNOWLEDGMENTS

Well, my Belroy boys and babes, this novella marks the end of our journey through Casolla. Thank you all so much for coming on this adventure with us. *Into the Churn* was originally supposed to be a stand-alone, and it's only through readers' ratings, reviews, and recommendations, that we were able to explore so much of this world. It was an absolute joy to write these books, and I hope you loved them as much as I do.

Special shout-out to my VSoc Street Team: Abby, Alex, Amanda, Brooke, Caitlin, Cassandra, Cassy, Dario, Em, Hannah, Jenn, Lee, Lily, Lorin, Marilee, Meghan, Megs, Rebecca, Ariana, Cleanbook_Reviews, Heather, Nade, Kate, & Lauren.

Without their help in hyping up this series and spreading the word, this book seriously wouldn't exist. They've been such an amazing source of excitement and support over the last three years, and it's been so much fun to (virtually) hang out with them!

As always, thanks to Whimsical Publishing for believing in this series and making it beautiful. Also huge thanks to Brogan for bringing the audiobooks to life (they are chaffing blime and I love them to death.) Thanks as well to my critique partners, Caleb and Erin, who are always by my side (virtually) to whip my drafts into shape.

And the last thank you goes to my amazing family—to my husband, parents, and fledgling book dragons for always supporting me as I obsessed over these worlds and characters. I love you all to Casolla and back again, and I can't wait to see where our adventures take us next.

It's always hard to say goodbye to a series—to these characters and the fantastical world they live in—and I will miss the chaff out of the Casolla universe. (I'm not crying; you're crying!) But there are other worlds to explore, characters to meet, and adventures to be had.

So, let's raise our glasses (umbrella drinks, of course) to wherever the storm winds may take us next, and I'll hope to see you there.

ABOUT THE AUTHOR

Hayley Reese Chow is the award-winning author of Odriel's Heirs, Into the Churn, and other upcoming YA adventures. When not head over heels in a bookish world, she's also a full-time engineer, USAF reservist, avid traveler, and super nerd. Hayley currently dodges hurricanes in Florida with two small ninjas, her long-suffering husband, and her miniature rage-hound. To see what she's working on next, check out hayleyreesechow.com or VSoc at @HayleyReeseChow.

instagram.com/hayleyreesechow

www.ingramcontent.com/pod-product-compliance
Lightning Source LLC
Chambersburg PA
CBHW020937180626
46814CB00003B/845
* 9 7 8 1 9 9 8 1 9 5 3 8 1 *